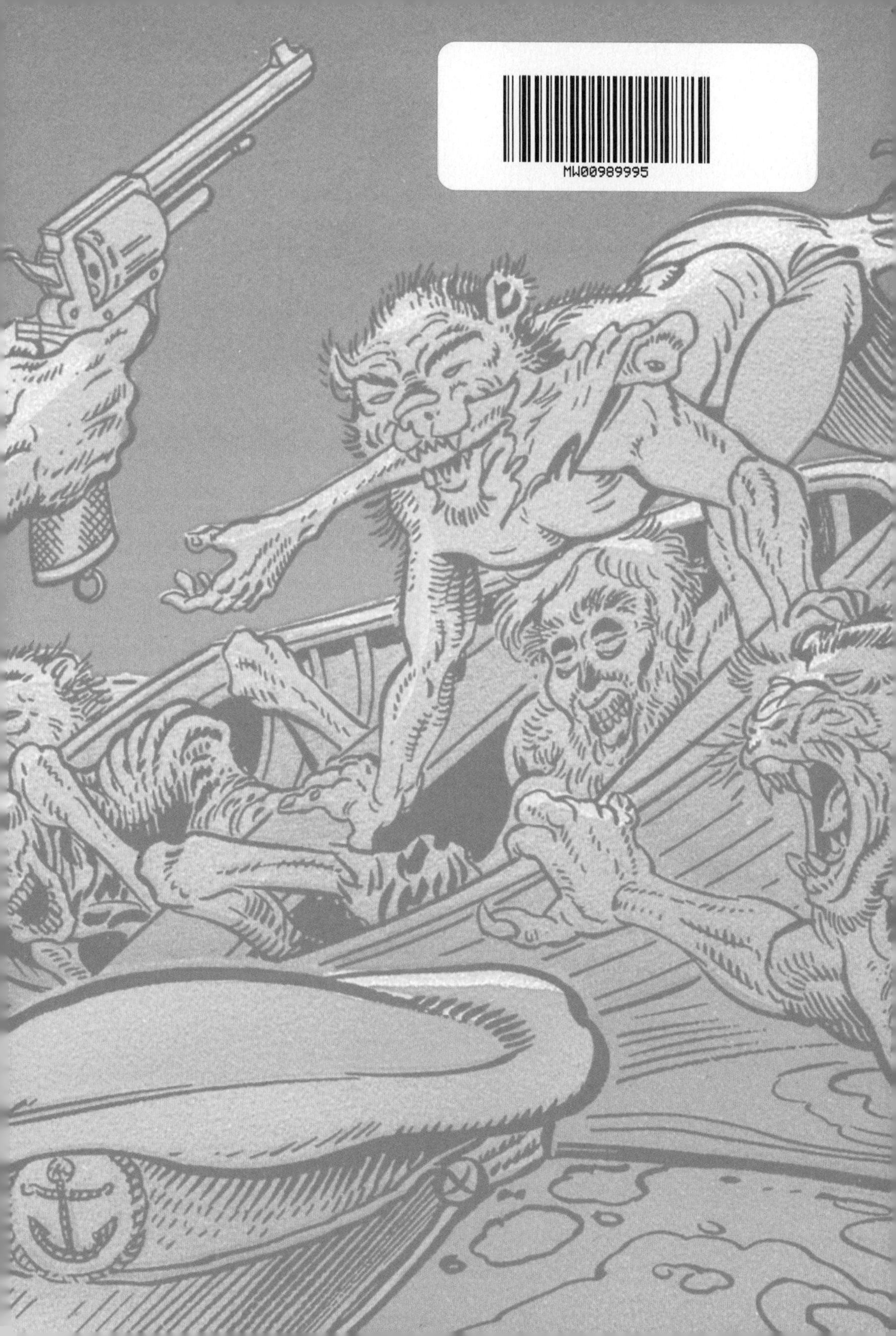

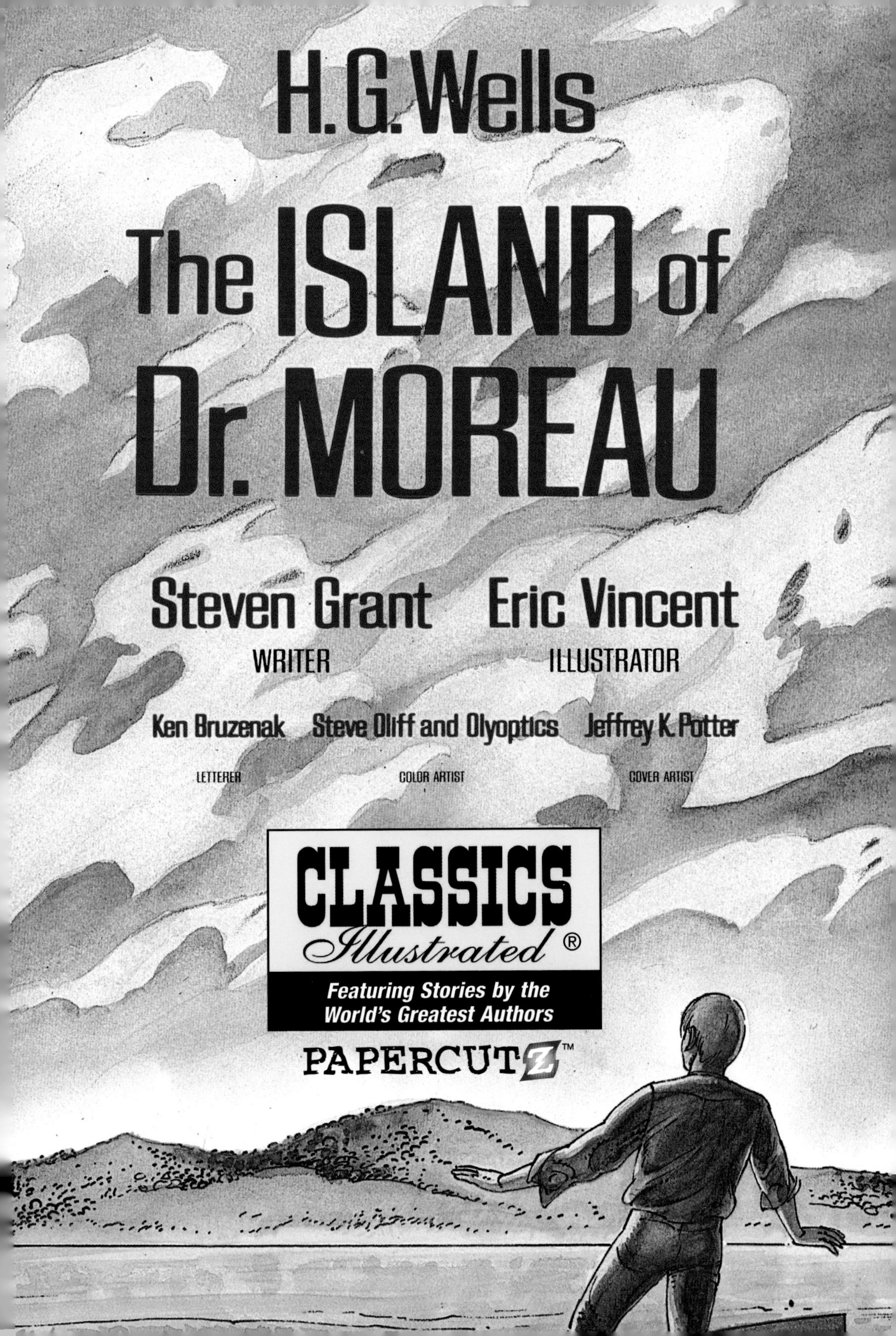

H. G. Wells

The ISLAND of Dr. MOREAU

Steven Grant
WRITER

Eric Vincent
ILLUSTRATOR

Ken Bruzenak
LETTERER

Steve Oliff and Olyoptics
COLOR ARTIST

Jeffrey K. Potter
COVER ARTIST

CLASSICS Illustrated®
Featuring Stories by the World's Greatest Authors

PAPERCUTZ™

CLASSICS ILLUSTRATED GRAPHIC NOVELS AVAILABLE FROM PAPERCUTZ

#1 "Great Expectations"

#2 "The Invisible Man"

#3 "Through the Looking-Glass"

#4 "The Raven and Other Poems"

#5 "Hamlet"

#6 "The Scarlet Letter"

#7 "Dr. Jekyll & Mr. Hyde"

#8 "The Count of Monte Cristo"

#9 "The Jungle"

#10 "Cyrano de Bergerac"

#11 "The Devil's Dictionary and Other Works"

#12 "The Island of Doctor Moreau"

Coming April '11 #13 "Ivanhoe"

CLASSICS ILLUSTRATED graphic novels are available only in hardcover for $9.95 each, except #8-13, $9.99 each. Please add $4.00 for postage and handling for the first book, add $1.00 for each additional book. MC, Visa, Amex accepted or make check payable to NBM Publishing.
Send to: Papercutz, 1200 Rte. 523, Flemington, NJ, 08822 • 1-800-886-1223

WWW.PAPERCUTZ.COM

Featuring Stories by the World's Greatest Authors

#12

THE
ISLAND
OF
DR. MOREAU

By H.G. Wells
Adapted by Steven Grant & Eric Vincent

PAPERCUTZ™
New York

The impressive literary achievements of H.G. Wells were extremely diverse, yet he was always best known for his "scientific romances." **The Island of Dr. Moreau** (1896) was the third in Wells's long line of scientific romances, preceded by *The Time Machine* and *The Wonderful Visit* (1895), and followed by such works as *The Invisible Man* (1897), *The War of the Worlds* (1898), and *The First Men in the Moon* (1901). With these novels, Wells defined a popular new literary genre that is now known as science fiction. Wells's fantasies were always distinguished by their critical, as well as popular, success. While readers delighted in the imaginative stories, critics and scholars were intrigued by Wells's blend of satire, warnings about the possible dangers of new scientific advancements, and predictions of new social orders. Wells's preoccupation with both social and scientific progress stemmed from his part in the nineteenth century's great scientific/religious debates, in which the ethics and morals of the two estates were argued and questioned. Wells took a middle ground in that philosophical struggle. He believed in the potential of science to help create a utopia, but, at the same time, he recognized the disaster that could result from the misuse of knowledge. He believed in social order, but thought that humanity had to be ready to shed old systems in order to achieve a higher standard of existence. That conflict is what makes **The Island of Dr. Moreau** so compelling, so frightening – "an atrocious miracle," as Jorge Luis Borges has called it. Science's promise of a better life is shattered when Moreau, a man of uncompromising logic, abuses his knowledge. At the same time, the island's social order unravels when its unreasoning creatures cannot recognize that their cultural structure is the source of their misery. To survive, Wells argued, we must carefully consider the potential effects of any action *or* inaction. As dark as his vision is in **The Island of Dr. Moreau**, there remains a light, a caution – a lesson.

The Island of Dr. Moreau
By H.G. Wells
Adapted by Steven Grant
and Eric Vincent
Wade Roberts, Original Editorial Director
Alex Wald, Original Art Director
Production by Chris Nelson & Shelly Sterner
Classics Illustrated Historians – John Haufe and
William B. Jones Jr.
Associate Editor – Michael Petranek
Jim Salicrup
Editor-in-Chief

ISBN: 978-1-59707-235-9

Copyright © 1990 First Classics, Inc.
The Classics Illustrated name and logo is
Copyright © 2011 First Classics, Inc.
All Rights Reserved. By permission of Jack
Lake Productions Inc.
Classics Illustrated ® is a registered trademark
of the Frawley Corporation.
Editorial matter copyright © 2011 Papercutz.

Printed in China
September 2010 by Regent Printing
6/F Hang Tung Resource Centre
No. 18 A Kung Ngam Village Road
Shau Kei Wan, Hong Kong

Distributed by Macmillan.

First Printing

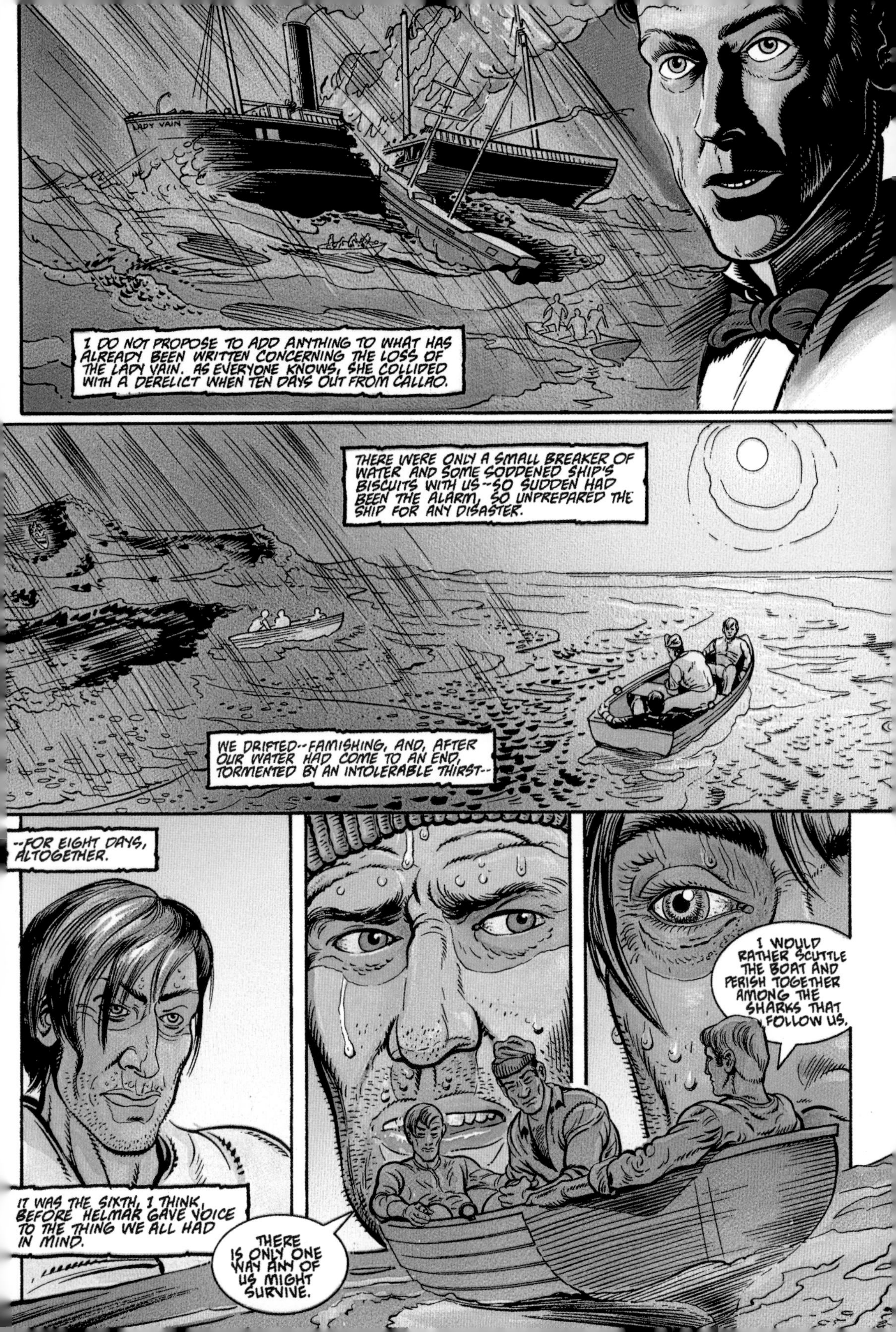
LADY VAIN
I DO NOT PROPOSE TO ADD ANYTHING TO WHAT HAS ALREADY BEEN WRITTEN CONCERNING THE LOSS OF THE LADY VAIN. AS EVERYONE KNOWS, SHE COLLIDED WITH A DERELICT WHEN TEN DAYS OUT FROM CALLAO.
THERE WERE ONLY A SMALL BREAKER OF WATER AND SOME SODDENED SHIP'S BISCUITS WITH US--SO SUDDEN HAD BEEN THE ALARM, SO UNPREPARED THE SHIP FOR ANY DISASTER.
WE DRIFTED--FAMISHING, AND, AFTER OUR WATER HAD COME TO AN END, TORMENTED BY AN INTOLERABLE THIRST--
--FOR EIGHT DAYS, ALTOGETHER.
IT WAS THE SIXTH, I THINK, BEFORE HELMAR GAVE VOICE TO THE THING WE ALL HAD IN MIND.
THERE IS ONLY ONE WAY ANY OF US MIGHT SURVIVE.
I WOULD RATHER SCUTTLE THE BOAT AND PERISH TOGETHER AMONG THE SHARKS THAT FOLLOW US.

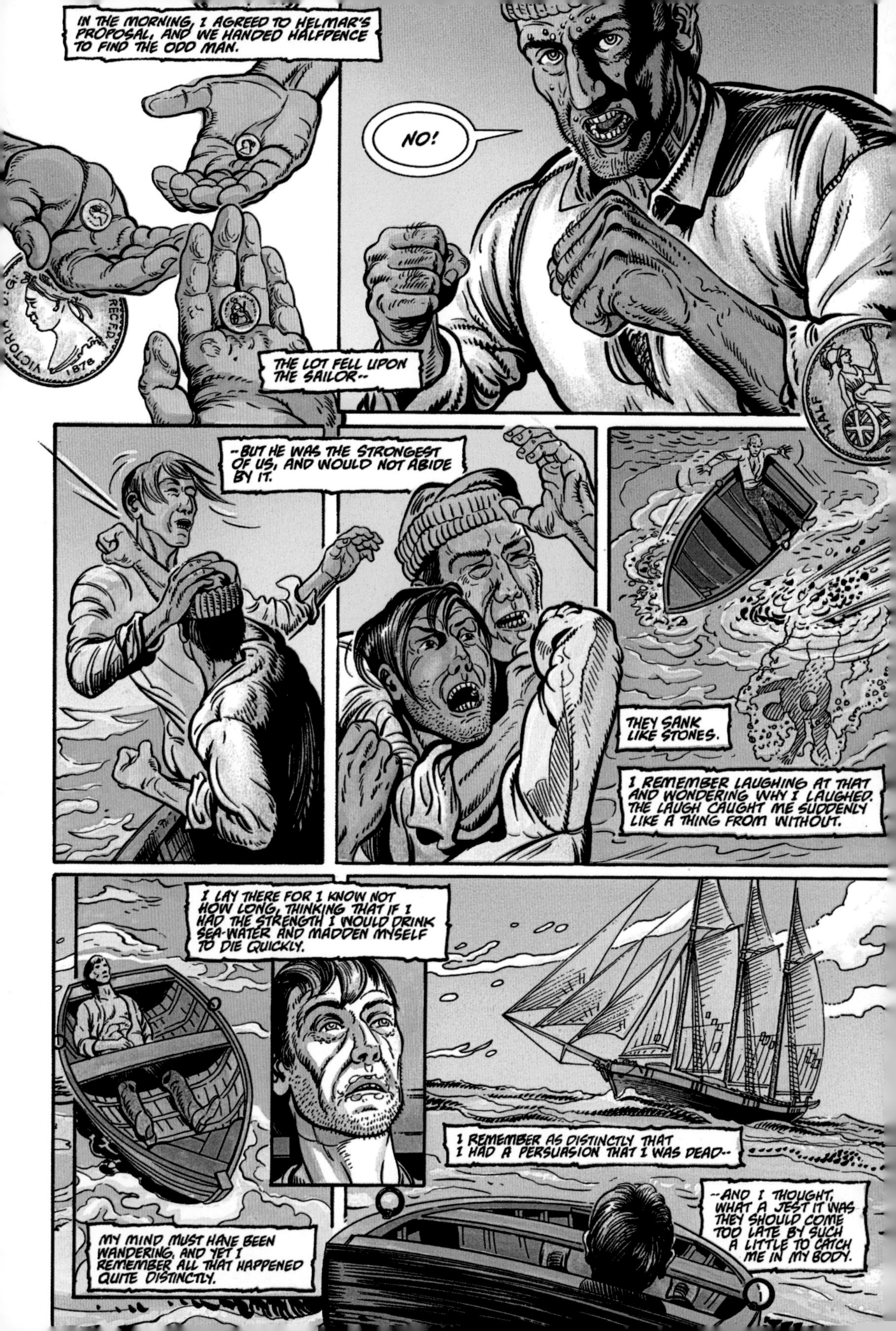
IN THE MORNING, I AGREED TO HELMAR'S PROPOSAL, AND WE HANDED HALFPENCE TO FIND THE ODD MAN.
VICTORIA D: G: BRIT: REG: F: D: 1878
THE LOT FELL UPON THE SAILOR--
NO!
HALF
--BUT HE WAS THE STRONGEST OF US, AND WOULD NOT ABIDE BY IT.
THEY SANK LIKE STONES.
I REMEMBER LAUGHING AT THAT AND WONDERING WHY I LAUGHED. THE LAUGH CAUGHT ME SUDDENLY LIKE A THING FROM WITHOUT.
I LAY THERE FOR I KNOW NOT HOW LONG, THINKING THAT IF I HAD THE STRENGTH I WOULD DRINK SEA-WATER AND MADDEN MYSELF TO DIE QUICKLY.
I REMEMBER AS DISTINCTLY THAT I HAD A PERSUASION THAT I WAS DEAD--
--AND I THOUGHT, WHAT A JEST IT WAS THEY SHOULD COME TOO LATE BY SUCH A LITTLE TO CATCH ME IN MY BODY.
MY MIND MUST HAVE BEEN WANDERING, AND YET I REMEMBER ALL THAT HAPPENED QUITE DISTINCTLY.

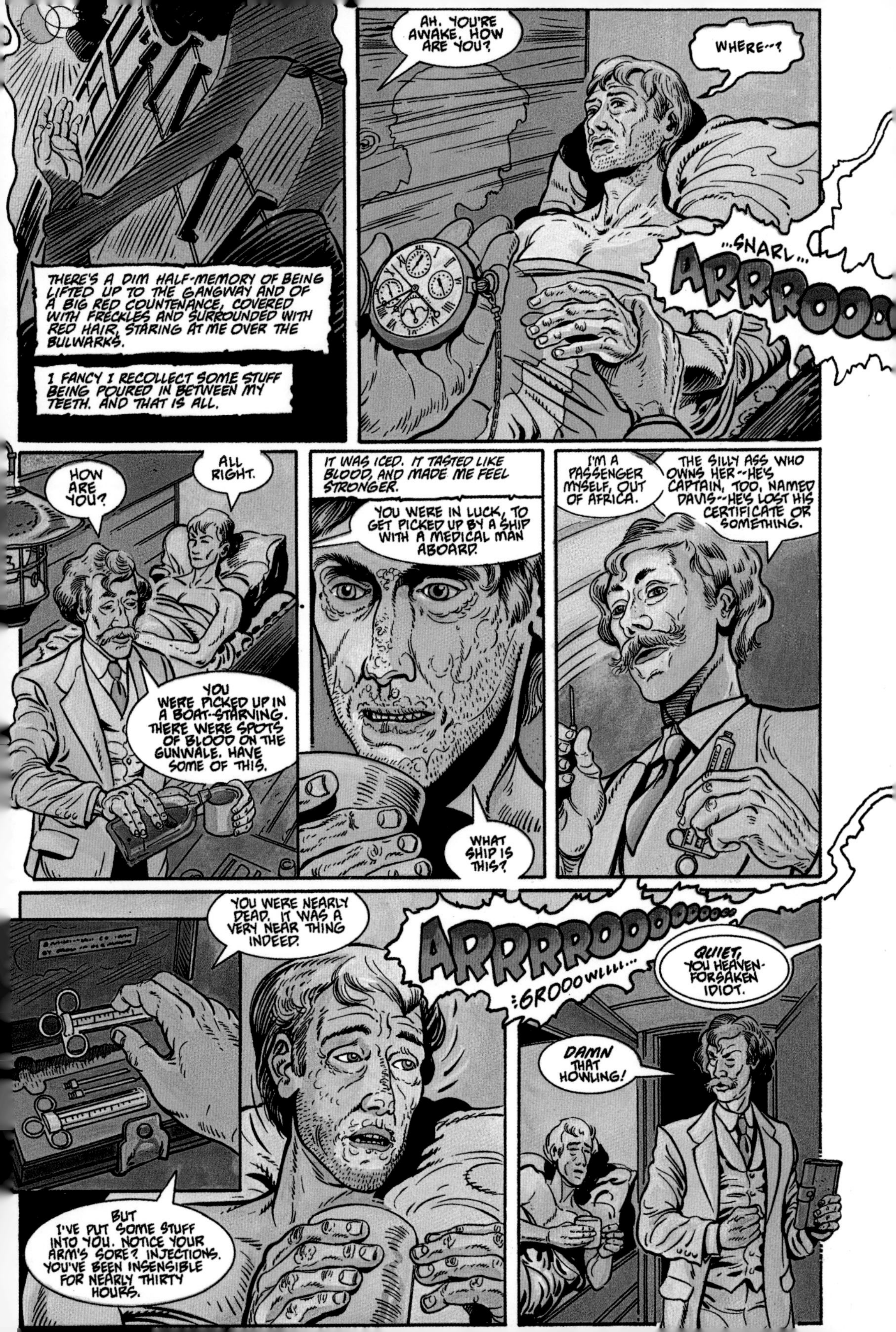
THERE'S A DIM HALF-MEMORY OF BEING LIFTED UP TO THE GANGWAY AND OF A BIG RED COUNTENANCE, COVERED WITH FRECKLES AND SURROUNDED WITH RED HAIR, STARING AT ME OVER THE BULWARKS.
I FANCY I RECOLLECT SOME STUFF BEING POURED IN BETWEEN MY TEETH. AND THAT IS ALL.
AH. YOU'RE AWAKE. HOW ARE YOU?
WHERE--?
...SNARL...
ARRROOO
HOW ARE YOU?
ALL RIGHT.
YOU WERE PICKED UP IN A BOAT--STARVING. THERE WERE SPOTS OF BLOOD ON THE GUNWALE. HAVE SOME OF THIS.
IT WAS ICED. IT TASTED LIKE BLOOD, AND MADE ME FEEL STRONGER.
YOU WERE IN LUCK, TO GET PICKED UP BY A SHIP WITH A MEDICAL MAN ABOARD.
WHAT SHIP IS THIS?
I'M A PASSENGER MYSELF, OUT OF AFRICA.
THE SILLY ASS WHO OWNS HER--HE'S CAPTAIN, TOO, NAMED DAVIS--HE'S LOST HIS CERTIFICATE OR SOMETHING.
YOU WERE NEARLY DEAD. IT WAS A VERY NEAR THING INDEED.
BUT I'VE PUT SOME STUFF INTO YOU. NOTICE YOUR ARM'S SORE? INJECTIONS. YOU'VE BEEN INSENSIBLE FOR NEARLY THIRTY HOURS.
ARRRROOOOOOOOOO
GROOOWLLLL...
QUIET, YOU HEAVEN-FORSAKEN IDIOT.
DAMN THAT HOWLING!

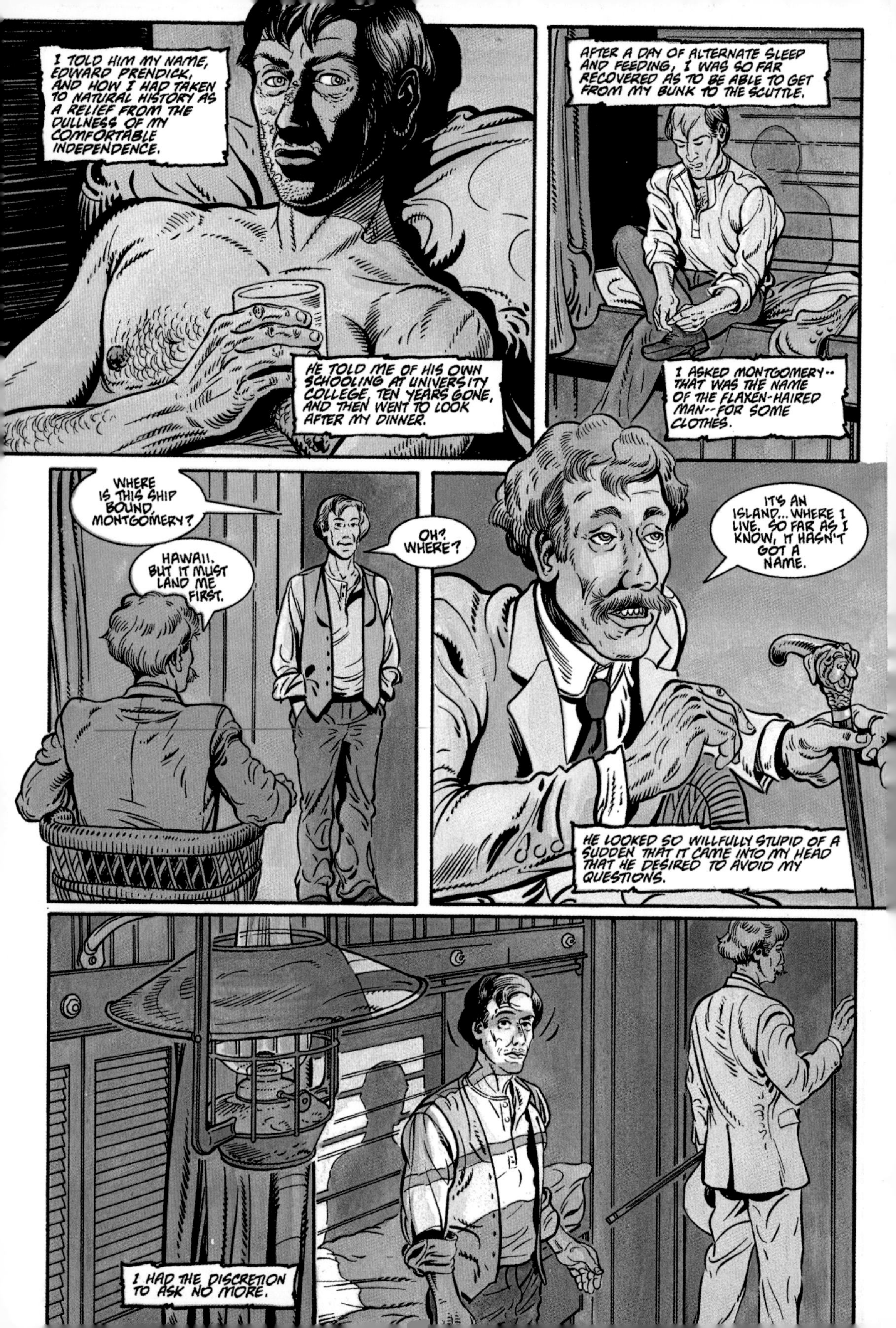
I TOLD HIM MY NAME, EDWARD PRENDICK, AND HOW I HAD TAKEN TO NATURAL HISTORY AS A RELIEF FROM THE DULLNESS OF MY COMFORTABLE INDEPENDENCE.
HE TOLD ME OF HIS OWN SCHOOLING AT UNIVERSITY COLLEGE, TEN YEARS GONE, AND THEN WENT TO LOOK AFTER MY DINNER.
AFTER A DAY OF ALTERNATE SLEEP AND FEEDING, I WAS SO FAR RECOVERED AS TO BE ABLE TO GET FROM MY BUNK TO THE SCUTTLE.
I ASKED MONTGOMERY--THAT WAS THE NAME OF THE FLAXEN-HAIRED MAN--FOR SOME CLOTHES.
WHERE IS THIS SHIP BOUND, MONTGOMERY?
HAWAII. BUT IT MUST LAND ME FIRST.
OH? WHERE?
IT'S AN ISLAND... WHERE I LIVE. SO FAR AS I KNOW, IT HASN'T GOT A NAME.
HE LOOKED SO WILLFULLY STUPID OF A SUDDEN THAT IT CAME INTO MY HEAD THAT HE DESIRED TO AVOID MY QUESTIONS.
I HAD THE DISCRETION TO ASK NO MORE.

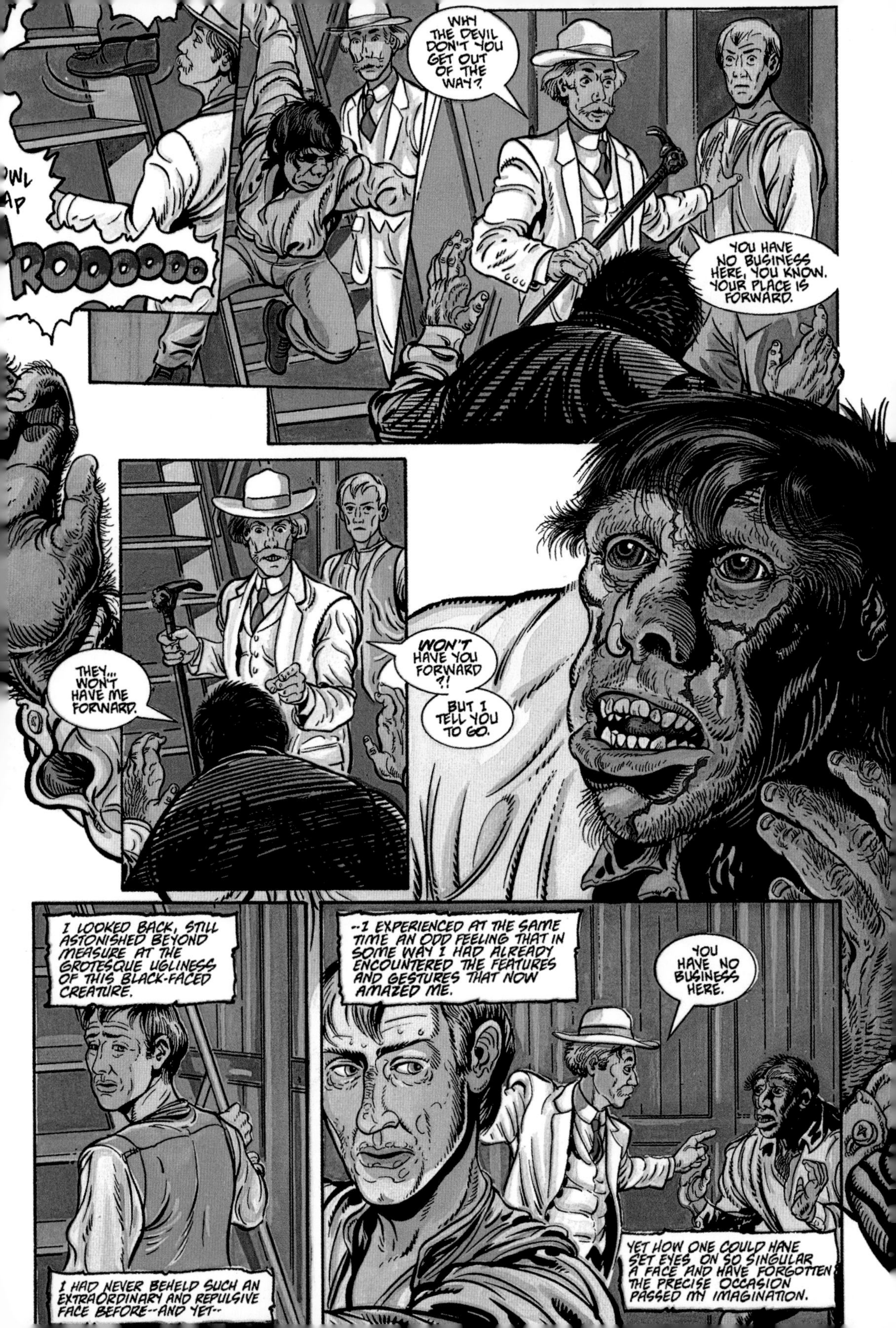
ROOOOOOO
WHY THE DEVIL DON'T YOU GET OUT OF THE WAY?
YOU HAVE NO BUSINESS HERE, YOU KNOW. YOUR PLACE IS FORWARD.
THEY... WON'T HAVE ME FORWARD.
WON'T HAVE YOU FORWARD?!
BUT I TELL YOU TO GO.
I LOOKED BACK, STILL ASTONISHED BEYOND MEASURE AT THE GROTESQUE UGLINESS OF THIS BLACK-FACED CREATURE.
I HAD NEVER BEHELD SUCH AN EXTRAORDINARY AND REPULSIVE FACE BEFORE--AND YET--
--I EXPERIENCED AT THE SAME TIME AN ODD FEELING THAT IN SOME WAY I HAD ALREADY ENCOUNTERED THE FEATURES AND GESTURES THAT NOW AMAZED ME.
YOU HAVE NO BUSINESS HERE.
YET HOW ONE COULD HAVE SET EYES ON SO SINGULAR A FACE AND HAVE FORGOTTEN THE PRECISE OCCASION PASSED MY IMAGINATION.

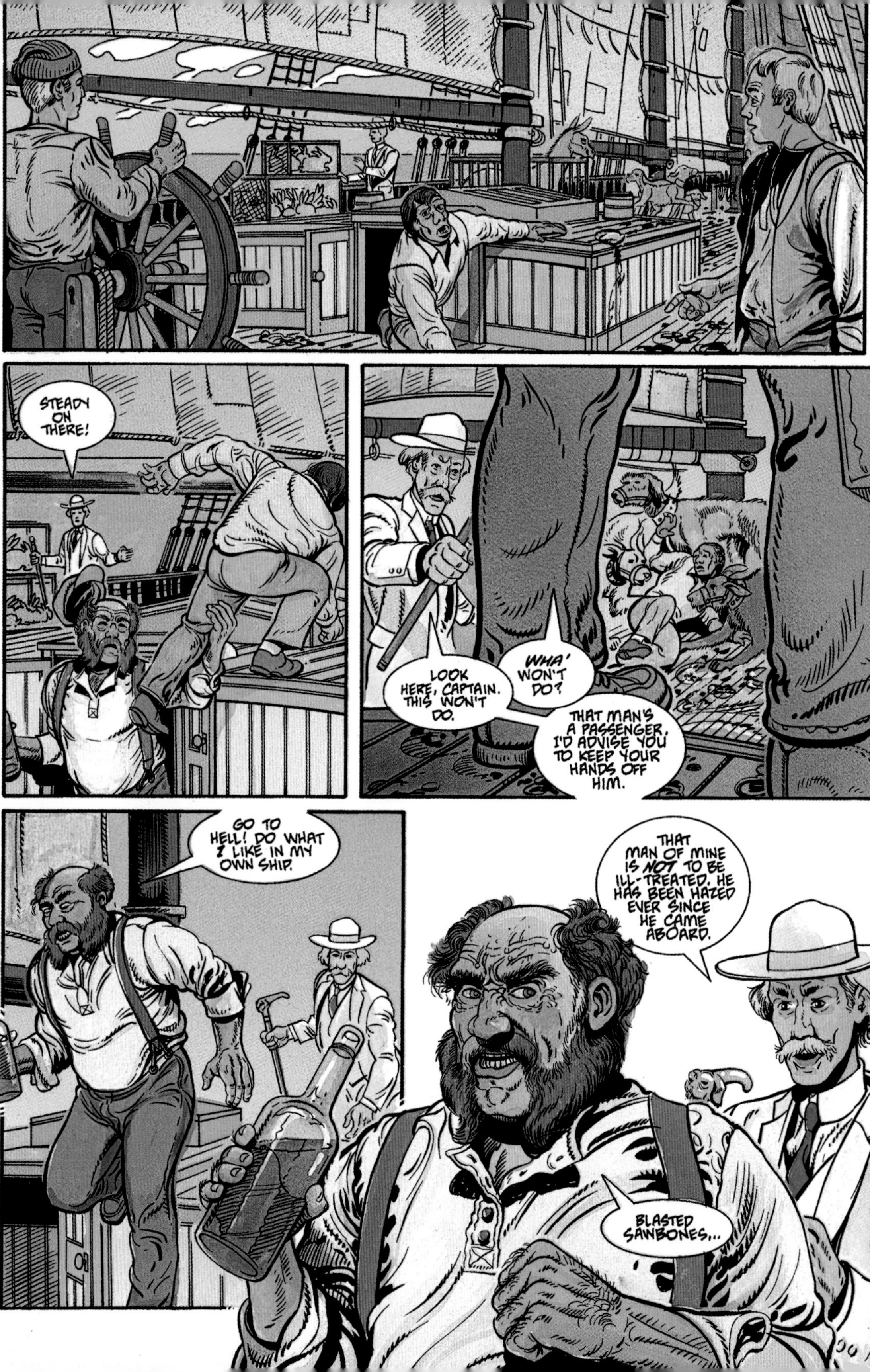
STEADY ON THERE!
LOOK HERE, CAPTAIN. THIS WON'T DO.
WHA' WON'T DO?
THAT MAN'S A PASSENGER. I'D ADVISE YOU TO KEEP YOUR HANDS OFF HIM.
GO TO HELL! DO WHAT I LIKE IN MY OWN SHIP.
THAT MAN OF MINE IS *NOT* TO BE ILL-TREATED. HE HAS BEEN HAZED EVER SINCE HE CAME ABOARD.
BLASTED SAWBONES,...

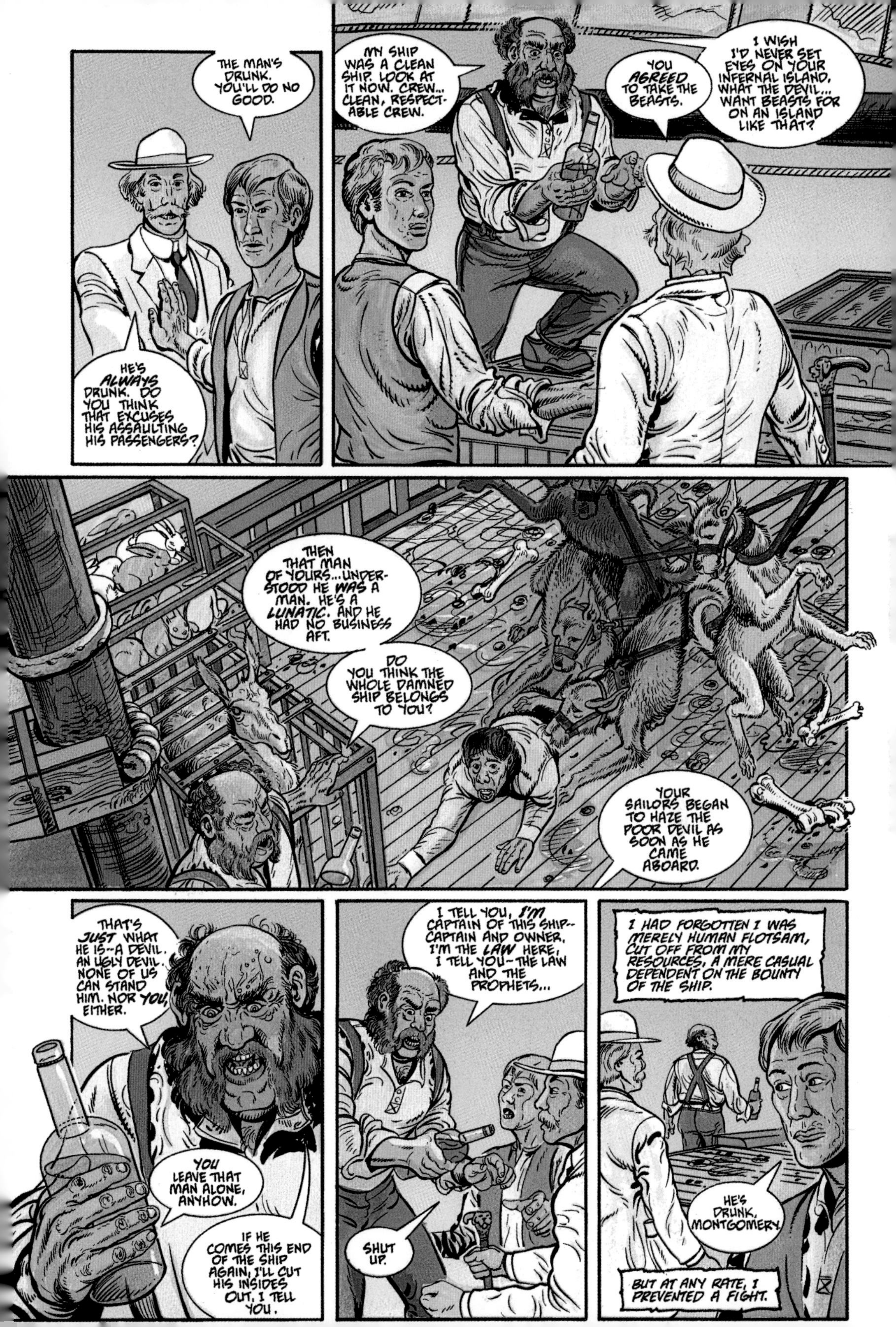
THE MAN'S DRUNK. YOU'LL DO NO GOOD.
HE'S ALWAYS DRUNK. DO YOU THINK THAT EXCUSES HIS ASSAULTING HIS PASSENGERS?
MY SHIP WAS A CLEAN SHIP. LOOK AT IT NOW. CREW... CLEAN, RESPECTABLE CREW.
YOU AGREED TO TAKE THE BEASTS.
I WISH I'D NEVER SET EYES ON YOUR INFERNAL ISLAND. WHAT THE DEVIL... WANT BEASTS FOR ON AN ISLAND LIKE THAT?
THEN THAT MAN OF YOURS... UNDERSTOOD HE WAS A MAN. HE'S A LUNATIC. AND HE HAD NO BUSINESS AFT.
DO YOU THINK THE WHOLE DAMNED SHIP BELONGS TO YOU?
YOUR SAILORS BEGAN TO HAZE THE POOR DEVIL AS SOON AS HE CAME ABOARD.
THAT'S JUST WHAT HE IS--A DEVIL. AN UGLY DEVIL. NONE OF US CAN STAND HIM. NOR YOU, EITHER.
YOU LEAVE THAT MAN ALONE, ANYHOW.
IF HE COMES THIS END OF THE SHIP AGAIN, I'LL CUT HIS INSIDES OUT, I TELL YOU.
I TELL YOU, I'M CAPTAIN OF THIS SHIP-- CAPTAIN AND OWNER. I'M THE LAW HERE, I TELL YOU-- THE LAW AND THE PROPHETS...
SHUT UP.
I HAD FORGOTTEN I WAS MERELY HUMAN FLOTSAM, CUT OFF FROM MY RESOURCES, A MERE CASUAL DEPENDENT ON THE BOUNTY OF THE SHIP.
HE'S DRUNK, MONTGOMERY.
BUT AT ANY RATE, I PREVENTED A FIGHT.

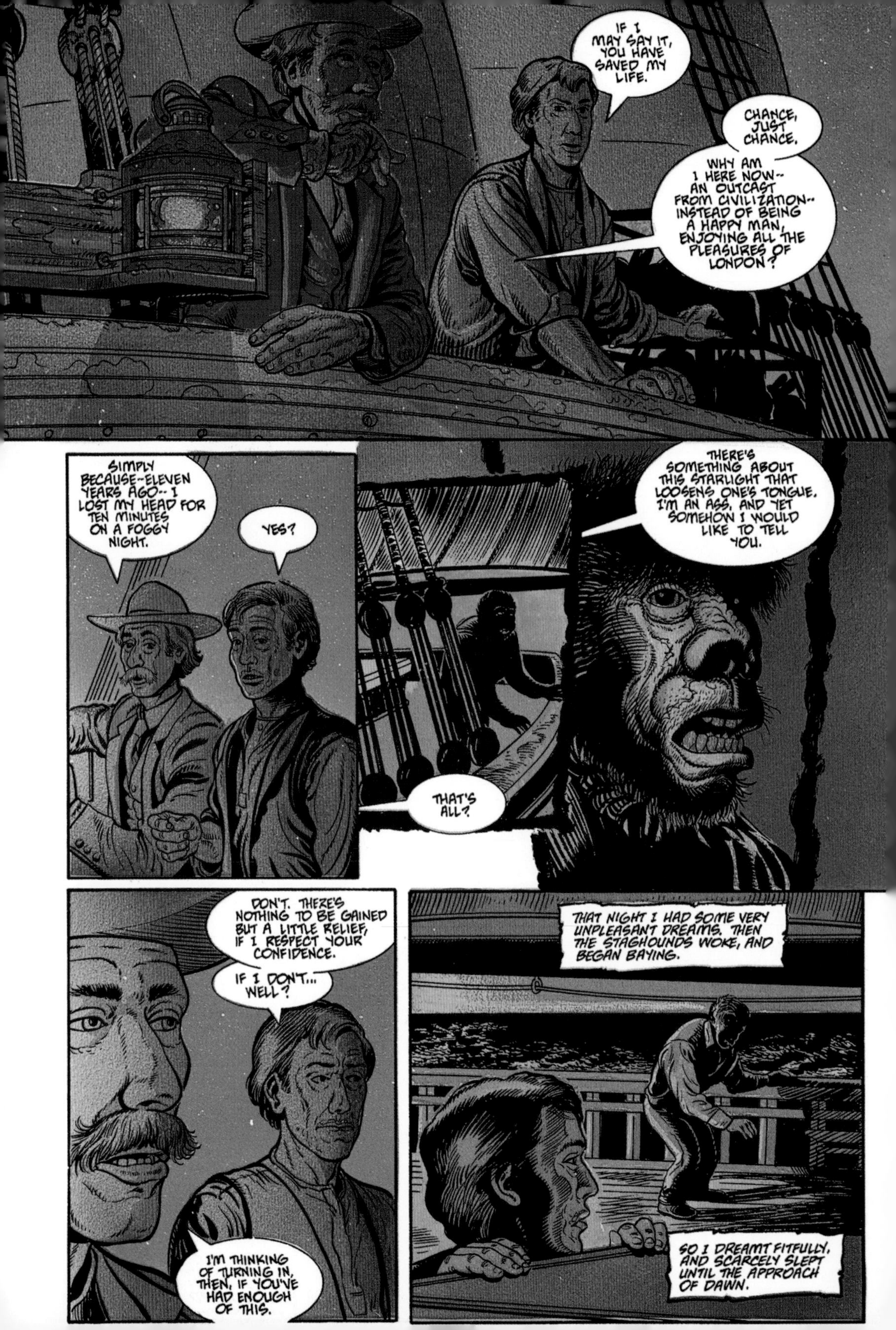
IF I MAY SAY IT, YOU HAVE SAVED MY LIFE.
CHANCE, JUST CHANCE.
WHY AM I HERE NOW-- AN OUTCAST FROM CIVILIZATION-- INSTEAD OF BEING A HAPPY MAN, ENJOYING ALL THE PLEASURES OF LONDON?
SIMPLY BECAUSE--ELEVEN YEARS AGO-- I LOST MY HEAD FOR TEN MINUTES ON A FOGGY NIGHT.
YES?
THERE'S SOMETHING ABOUT THIS STARLIGHT THAT LOOSENS ONE'S TONGUE. I'M AN ASS, AND YET SOMEHOW I WOULD LIKE TO TELL YOU.
THAT'S ALL?
DON'T. THERE'S NOTHING TO BE GAINED BUT A LITTLE RELIEF, IF I RESPECT YOUR CONFIDENCE.
IF I DON'T... WELL?
I'M THINKING OF TURNING IN, THEN, IF YOU'VE HAD ENOUGH OF THIS.
THAT NIGHT I HAD SOME VERY UNPLEASANT DREAMS. THEN THE STAGHOUNDS WOKE, AND BEGAN BAYING.
SO I DREAMT FITFULLY, AND SCARCELY SLEPT UNTIL THE APPROACH OF DAWN.

OVERBOARD WITH 'EM! WE'LL HAVE A CLEAN SHIP SOON OF THE WHOLE BILIN' OF 'EM!

HULLO! WHY, IT'S MISTER-- MISTER?

PRENDICK.

PRENDICK BE DAMNED! SHUT UP--THAT'S YOUR NAME, MISTER SHUT UP!

THAT WAY, MISTER BLASTED SHUT UP. THAT WAY.

WHAT DO YOU MEAN?

OVERBOARD, MISTER SHUT UP-- AND SHARP. WE'RE CLEANING THE WHOLE BLESSED SHIP OUT, AND OVERBOARD YOU GO.

CAN'T HAVE YOU.

YOU CAN'T HAVE ME?

THIS SHIP AIN'T FOR BEASTS AND CANNIBALS, AND WORSE THAN BEASTS, ANYMORE.

IF THEY CAN'T HAVE YOU, YOU GOES ADRIFT. I'VE DONE WITH THIS BLESSED ISLAND FOREVERMORE. AMEN!

MONTGOMERY!

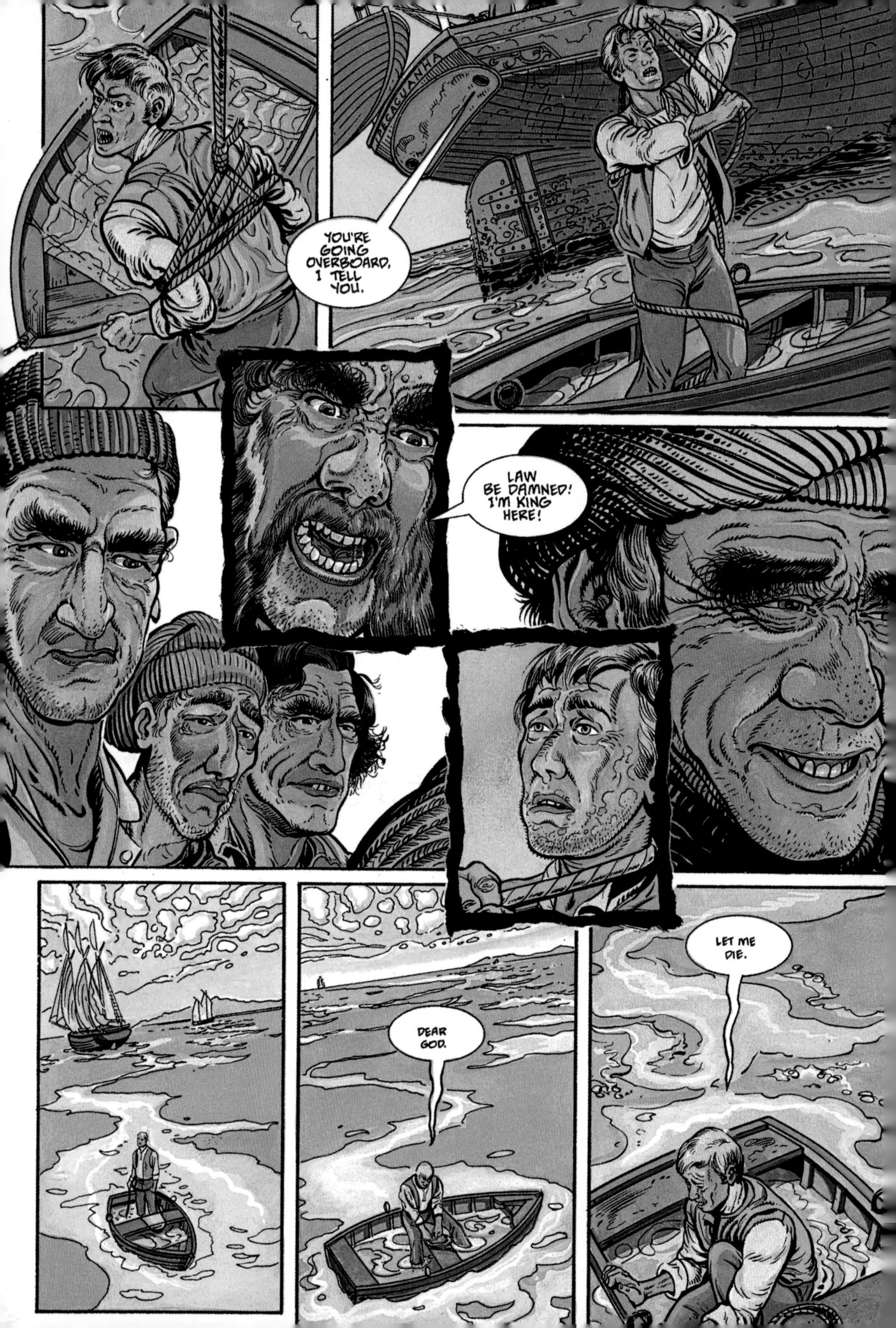
YOU'RE GOING OVERBOARD, I TELL YOU.
LAW BE DAMNED! I'M KING HERE!
DEAR GOD.
LET ME DIE.

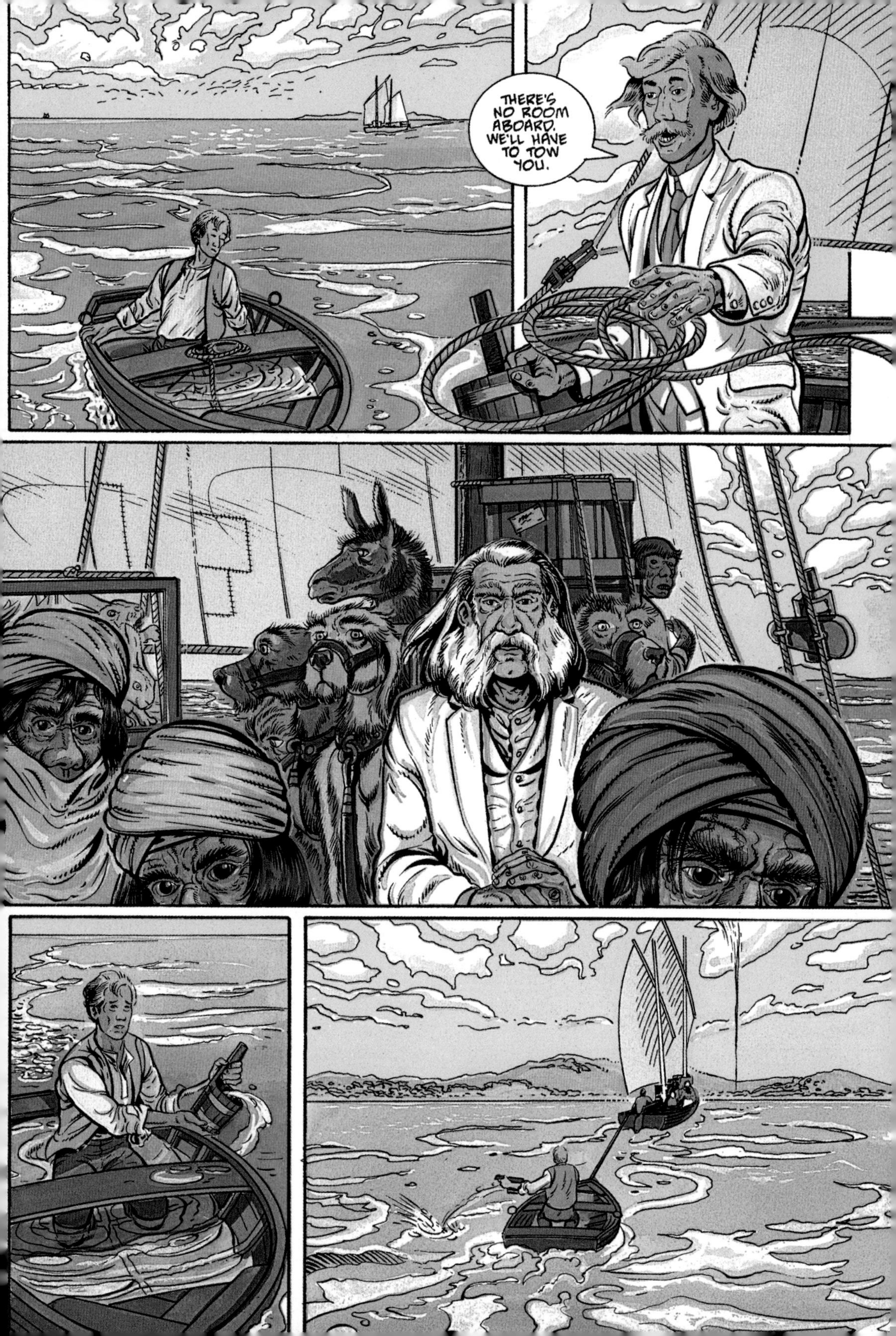
THERE'S NO ROOM ABOARD. WE'LL HAVE TO TOW YOU.

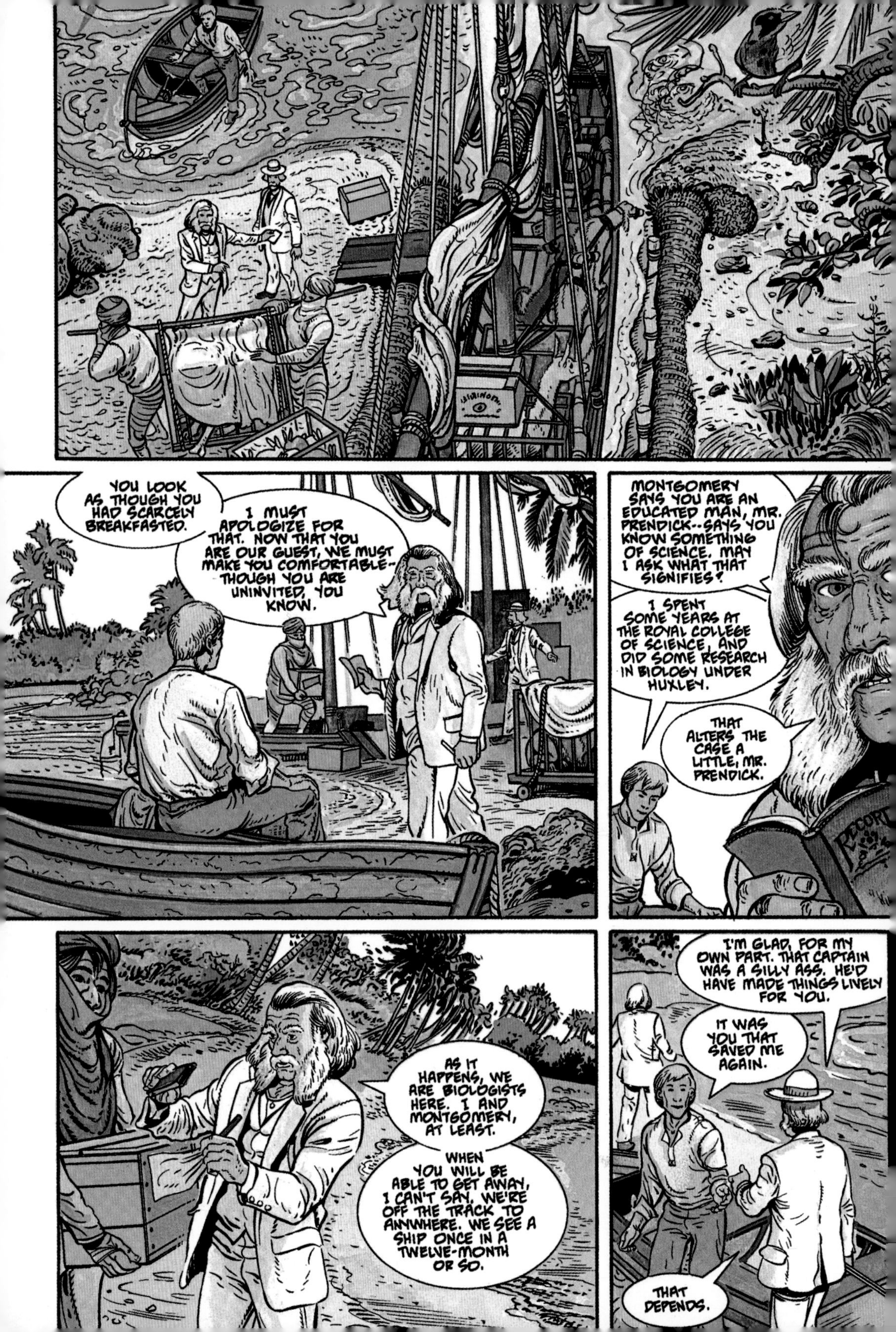
YOU LOOK AS THOUGH YOU HAD SCARCELY BREAKFASTED.
I MUST APOLOGIZE FOR THAT. NOW THAT YOU ARE OUR GUEST, WE MUST MAKE YOU COMFORTABLE--THOUGH YOU ARE UNINVITED, YOU KNOW.
MONTGOMERY SAYS YOU ARE AN EDUCATED MAN, MR. PRENDICK--SAYS YOU KNOW SOMETHING OF SCIENCE. MAY I ASK WHAT THAT SIGNIFIES?
I SPENT SOME YEARS AT THE ROYAL COLLEGE OF SCIENCE, AND DID SOME RESEARCH IN BIOLOGY UNDER HUXLEY.
THAT ALTERS THE CASE A LITTLE, MR. PRENDICK.
AS IT HAPPENS, WE ARE BIOLOGISTS HERE. I AND MONTGOMERY, AT LEAST.
WHEN YOU WILL BE ABLE TO GET AWAY, I CAN'T SAY. WE'RE OFF THE TRACK TO ANYWHERE. WE SEE A SHIP ONCE IN A TWELVE-MONTH OR SO.
I'M GLAD, FOR MY OWN PART. THAT CAPTAIN WAS A SILLY ASS. HE'D HAVE MADE THINGS LIVELY FOR YOU.
IT WAS YOU THAT SAVED ME AGAIN.
THAT DEPENDS.

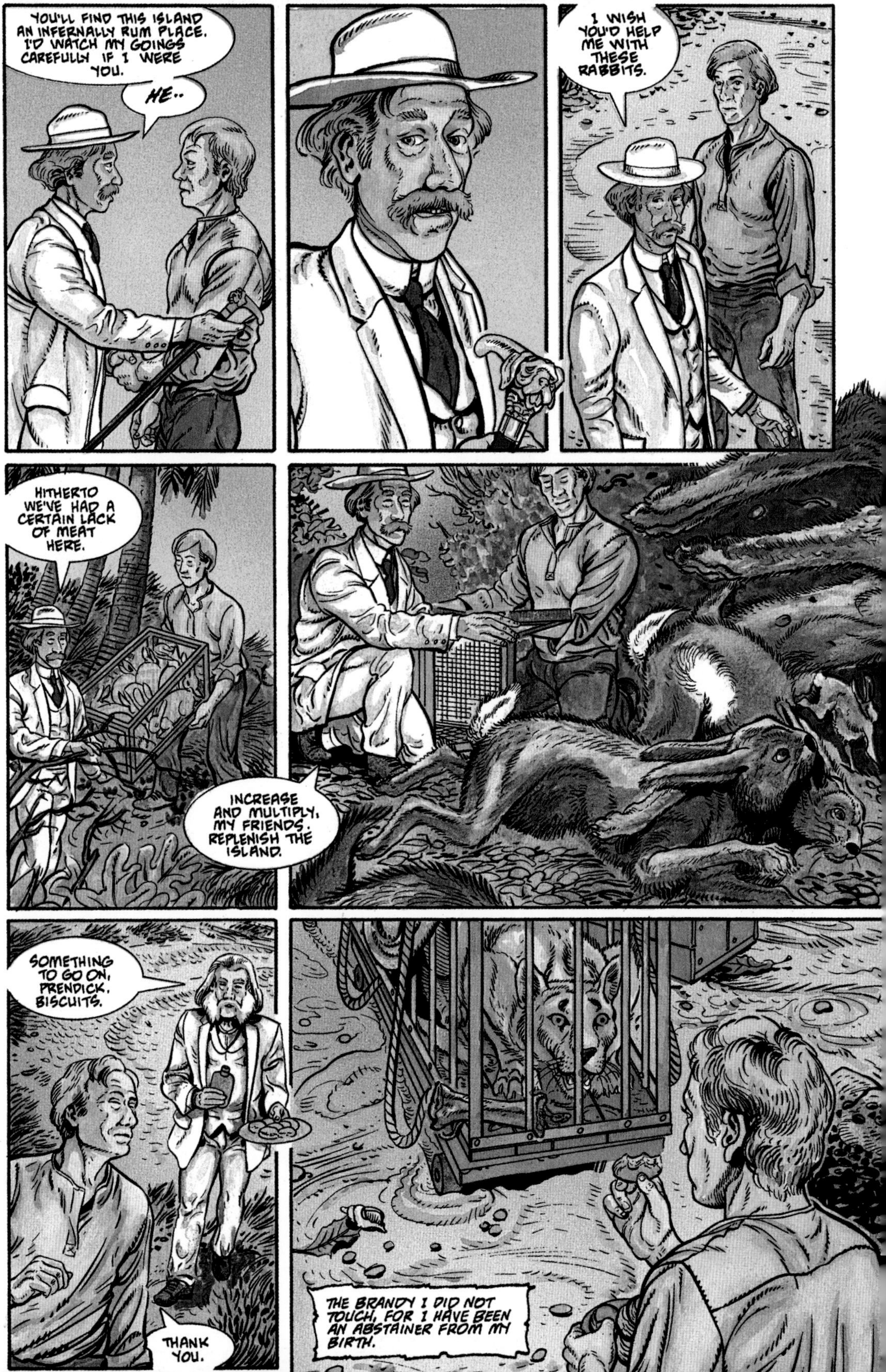
YOU'LL FIND THIS ISLAND AN INFERNALLY RUM PLACE. I'D WATCH MY GOINGS CAREFULLY IF I WERE YOU.
HE..
I WISH YOU'D HELP ME WITH THESE RABBITS.
HITHERTO WE'VE HAD A CERTAIN LACK OF MEAT HERE.
INCREASE AND MULTIPLY, MY FRIENDS. REPLENISH THE ISLAND.
SOMETHING TO GO ON, PRENDICK. BISCUITS.
THANK YOU.
THE BRANDY I DID NOT TOUCH, FOR I HAVE BEEN AN ABSTAINER FROM MY BIRTH.

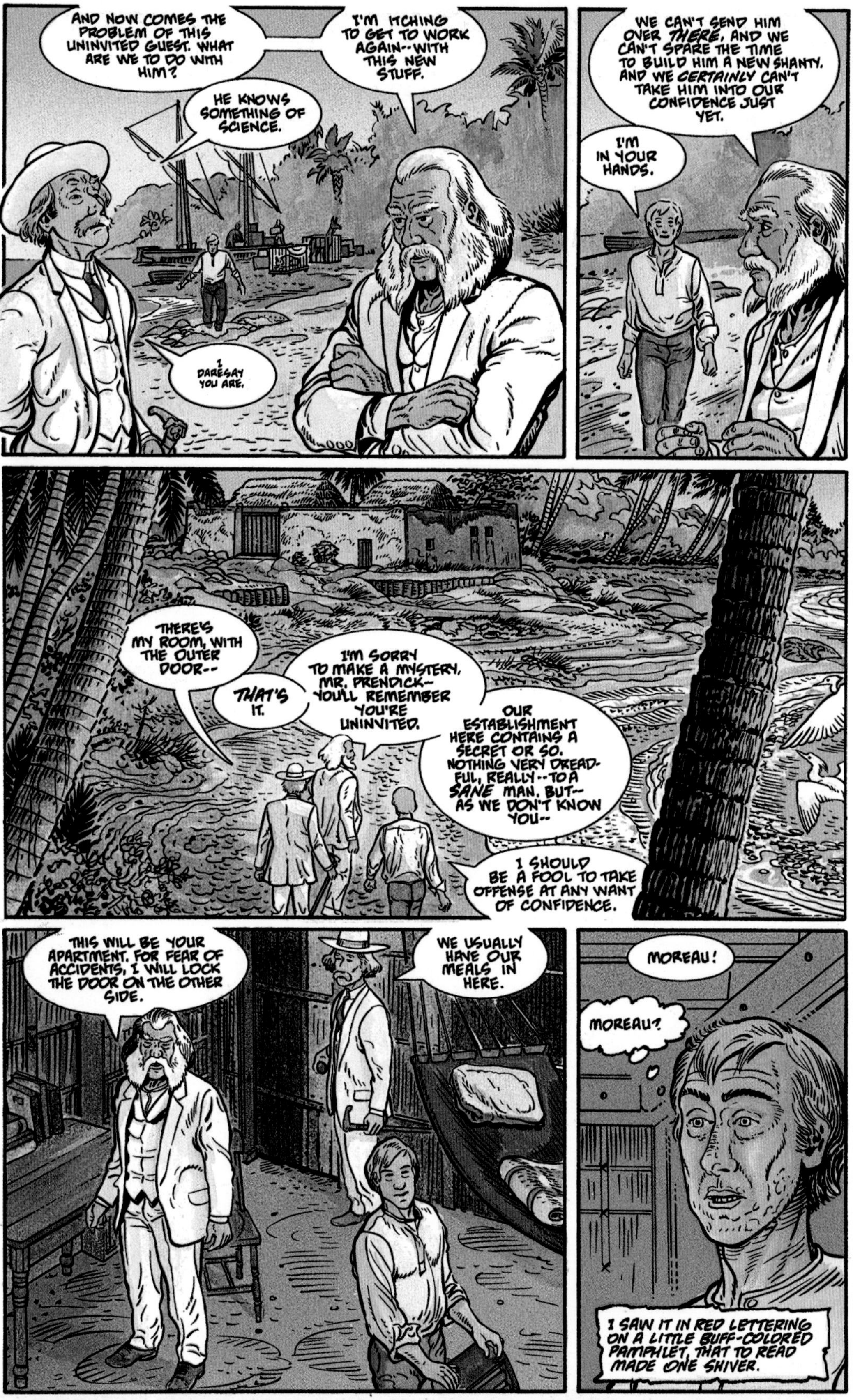
AND NOW COMES THE PROBLEM OF THIS UNINVITED GUEST. WHAT ARE WE TO DO WITH HIM?
I'M ITCHING TO GET TO WORK AGAIN--WITH THIS NEW STUFF.
HE KNOWS SOMETHING OF SCIENCE.
I DARESAY YOU ARE.
WE CAN'T SEND HIM OVER THERE, AND WE CAN'T SPARE THE TIME TO BUILD HIM A NEW SHANTY. AND WE CERTAINLY CAN'T TAKE HIM INTO OUR CONFIDENCE JUST YET.
I'M IN YOUR HANDS.
THERE'S MY ROOM, WITH THE OUTER DOOR--
THAT'S IT.
I'M SORRY TO MAKE A MYSTERY, MR. PRENDICK--YOU'LL REMEMBER YOU'RE UNINVITED.
OUR ESTABLISHMENT HERE CONTAINS A SECRET OR SO. NOTHING VERY DREADFUL, REALLY--TO A SANE MAN. BUT--AS WE DON'T KNOW YOU--
I SHOULD BE A FOOL TO TAKE OFFENSE AT ANY WANT OF CONFIDENCE.
THIS WILL BE YOUR APARTMENT. FOR FEAR OF ACCIDENTS, I WILL LOCK THE DOOR ON THE OTHER SIDE.
WE USUALLY HAVE OUR MEALS IN HERE.
MOREAU!
MOREAU?
I SAW IT IN RED LETTERING ON A LITTLE BUFF-COLORED PAMPHLET, THAT TO READ MADE ONE SHIVER.

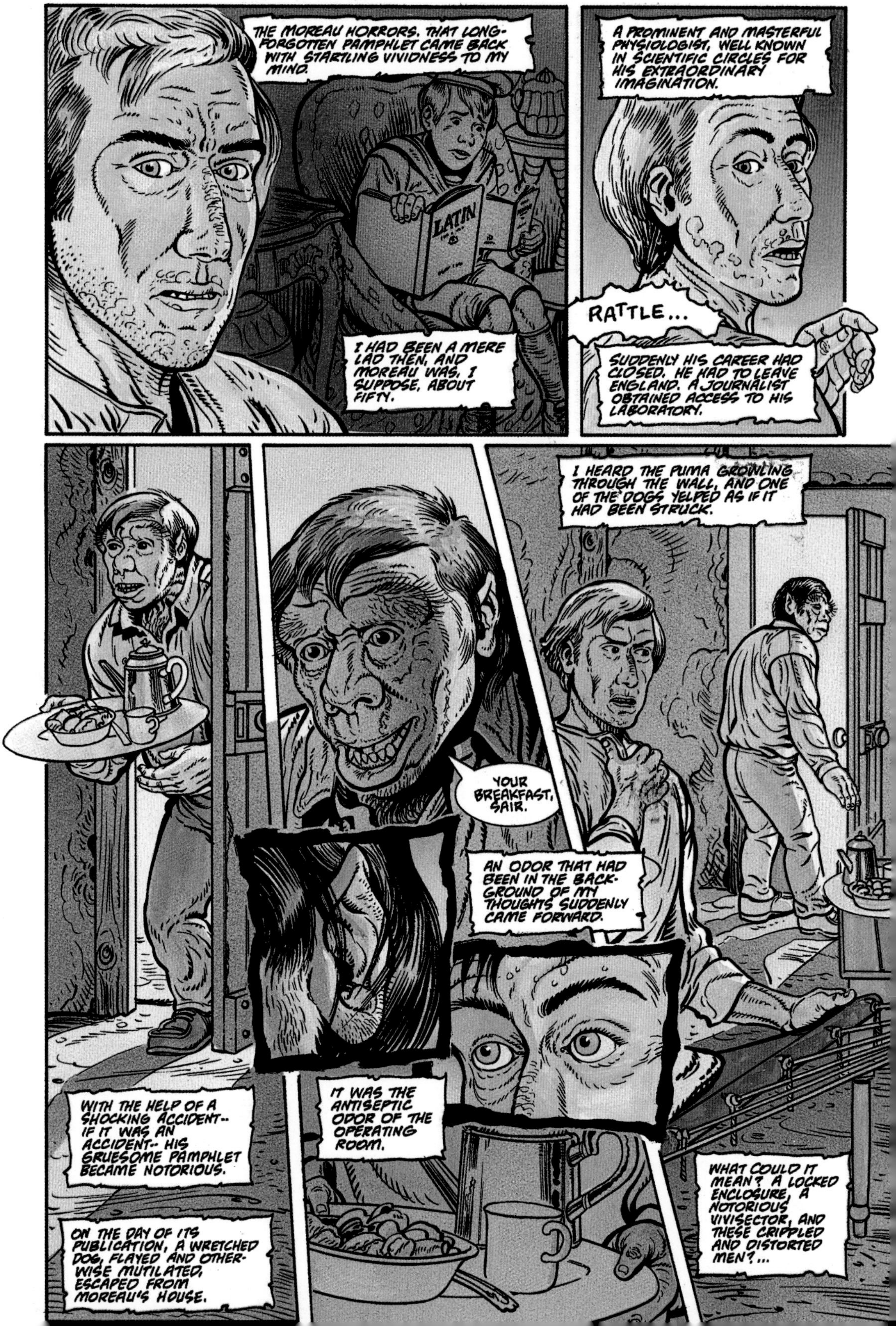
THE MOREAU HORRORS. THAT LONG-FORGOTTEN PAMPHLET CAME BACK WITH STARTLING VIVIDNESS TO MY MIND.
LATIN
I HAD BEEN A MERE LAD THEN, AND MOREAU WAS, I SUPPOSE, ABOUT FIFTY.
A PROMINENT AND MASTERFUL PHYSIOLOGIST, WELL KNOWN IN SCIENTIFIC CIRCLES FOR HIS EXTRAORDINARY IMAGINATION.
RATTLE...
SUDDENLY HIS CAREER HAD CLOSED. HE HAD TO LEAVE ENGLAND. A JOURNALIST OBTAINED ACCESS TO HIS LABORATORY.
YOUR BREAKFAST, SAIR.
WITH THE HELP OF A SHOCKING ACCIDENT-- IF IT WAS AN ACCIDENT-- HIS GRUESOME PAMPHLET BECAME NOTORIOUS.
ON THE DAY OF ITS PUBLICATION, A WRETCHED DOG, FLAYED AND OTHERWISE MUTILATED, ESCAPED FROM MOREAU'S HOUSE.
IT WAS THE ANTISEPTIC ODOR OF THE OPERATING ROOM.
AN ODOR THAT HAD BEEN IN THE BACKGROUND OF MY THOUGHTS SUDDENLY CAME FORWARD.
I HEARD THE PUMA GROWLING THROUGH THE WALL, AND ONE OF THE DOGS YELPED AS IF IT HAD BEEN STRUCK.
WHAT COULD IT MEAN? A LOCKED ENCLOSURE, A NOTORIOUS VIVISECTOR, AND THESE CRIPPLED AND DISTORTED MEN?...

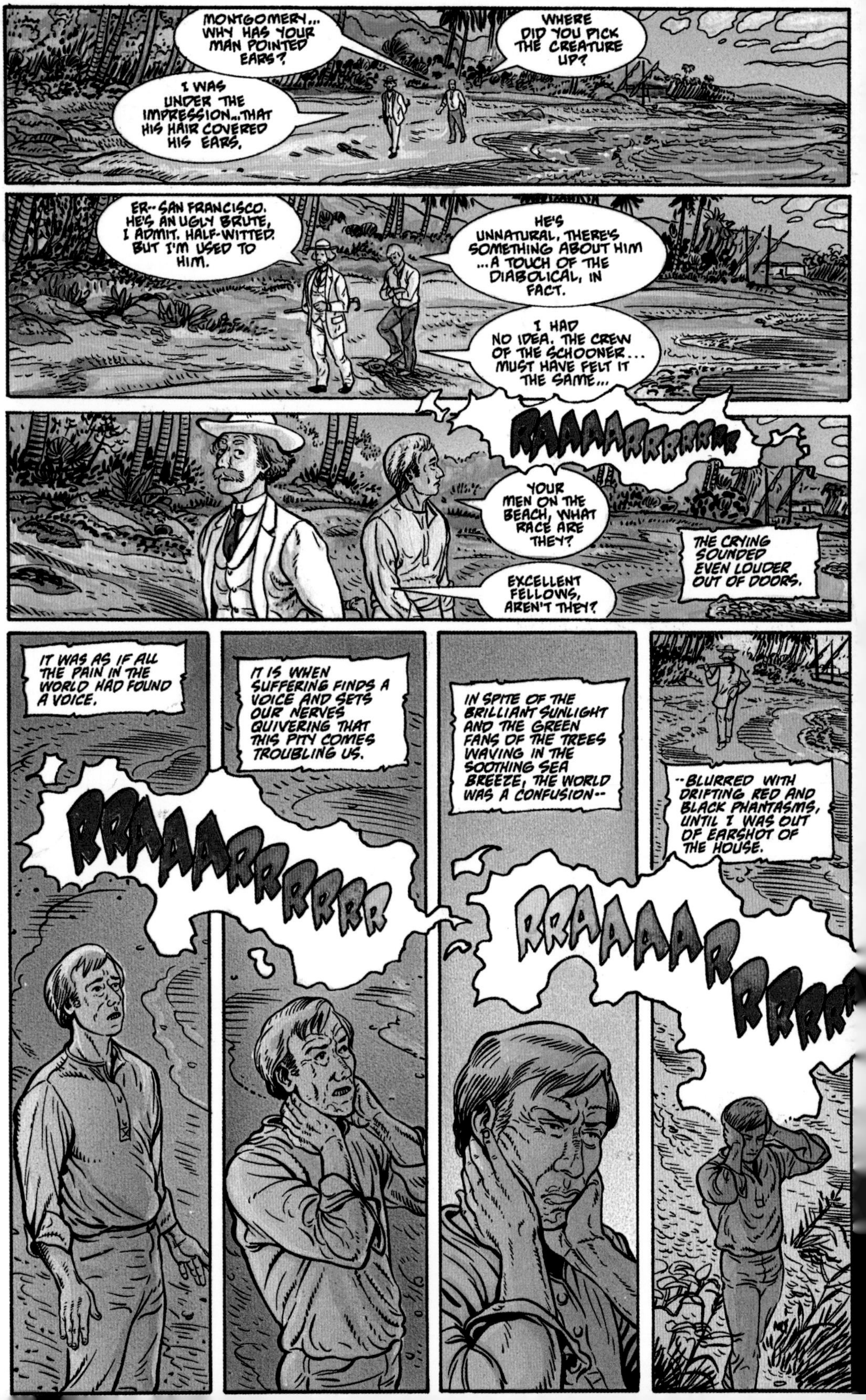
MONTGOMERY... WHY HAS YOUR MAN POINTED EARS?
I WAS UNDER THE IMPRESSION...THAT HIS HAIR COVERED HIS EARS.
WHERE DID YOU PICK THE CREATURE UP?
ER-- SAN FRANCISCO. HE'S AN UGLY BRUTE, I ADMIT. HALF-WITTED. BUT I'M USED TO HIM.
HE'S UNNATURAL, THERE'S SOMETHING ABOUT HIM ...A TOUCH OF THE DIABOLICAL, IN FACT.
I HAD NO IDEA. THE CREW OF THE SCHOONER... MUST HAVE FELT IT THE SAME...
RAAAARRRRRRR
YOUR MEN ON THE BEACH, WHAT RACE ARE THEY?
EXCELLENT FELLOWS, AREN'T THEY?
THE CRYING SOUNDED EVEN LOUDER OUT OF DOORS.
IT WAS AS IF ALL THE PAIN IN THE WORLD HAD FOUND A VOICE.
RRAAAARRRRRR
IT IS WHEN SUFFERING FINDS A VOICE AND SETS OUR NERVES QUIVERING THAT THIS PITY COMES TROUBLING US.
IN SPITE OF THE BRILLIANT SUNLIGHT AND THE GREEN FANS OF THE TREES WAVING IN THE SOOTHING SEA BREEZE, THE WORLD WAS A CONFUSION--
RRAAAAARRRRR
--BLURRED WITH DRIFTING RED AND BLACK PHANTASMS, UNTIL I WAS OUT OF EARSHOT OF THE HOUSE.

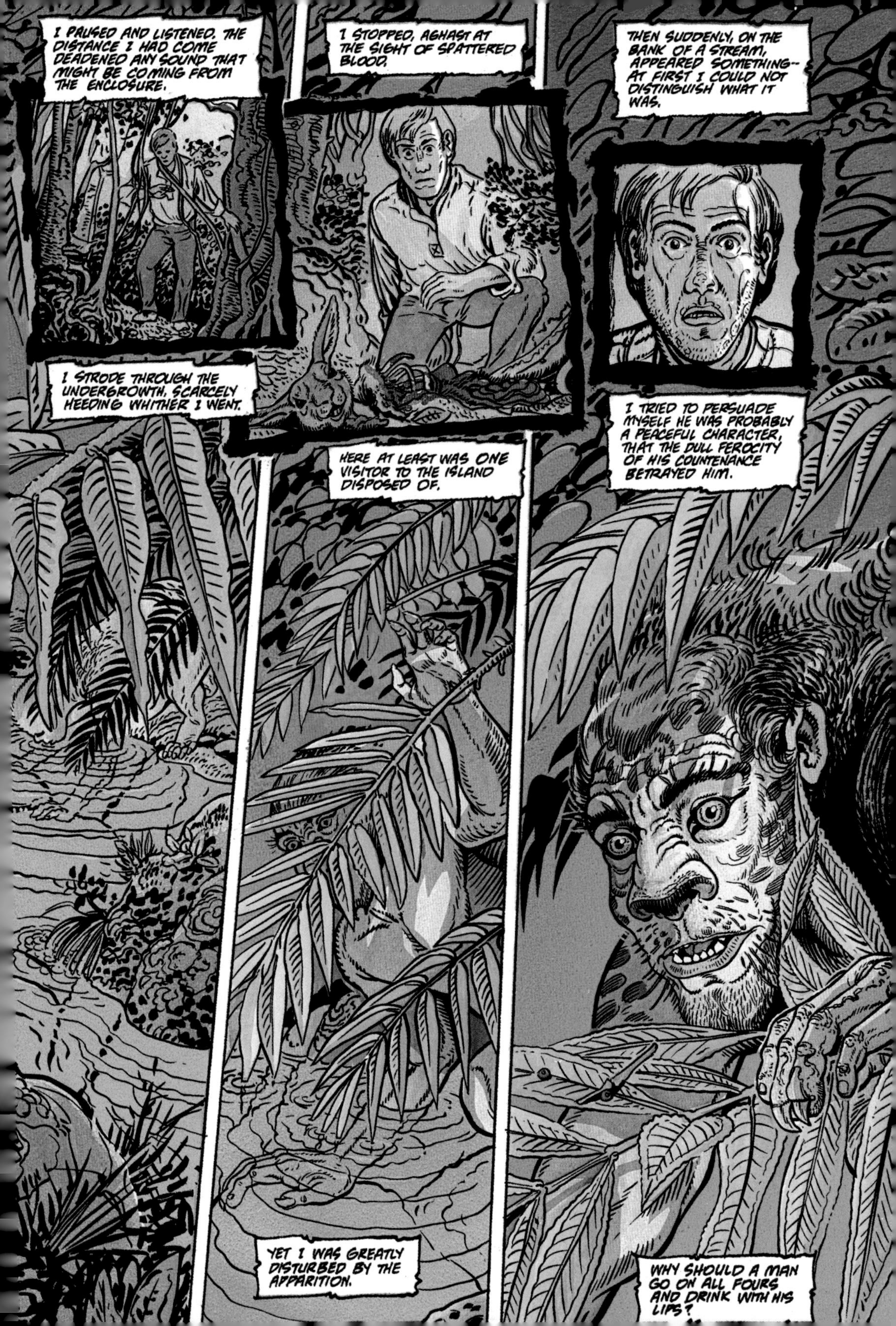
I PAUSED AND LISTENED. THE DISTANCE I HAD COME DEADENED ANY SOUND THAT MIGHT BE COMING FROM THE ENCLOSURE.
I STRODE THROUGH THE UNDERGROWTH, SCARCELY HEEDING WHITHER I WENT.
I STOPPED, AGHAST AT THE SIGHT OF SPATTERED BLOOD.
THEN SUDDENLY, ON THE BANK OF A STREAM, APPEARED SOMETHING-- AT FIRST I COULD NOT DISTINGUISH WHAT IT WAS.
HERE AT LEAST WAS ONE VISITOR TO THE ISLAND DISPOSED OF.
YET I WAS GREATLY DISTURBED BY THE APPARITION.
I TRIED TO PERSUADE MYSELF HE WAS PROBABLY A PEACEFUL CHARACTER, THAT THE DULL FEROCITY OF HIS COUNTENANCE BETRAYED HIM.
WHY SHOULD A MAN GO ON ALL FOURS AND DRINK WITH HIS LIPS?

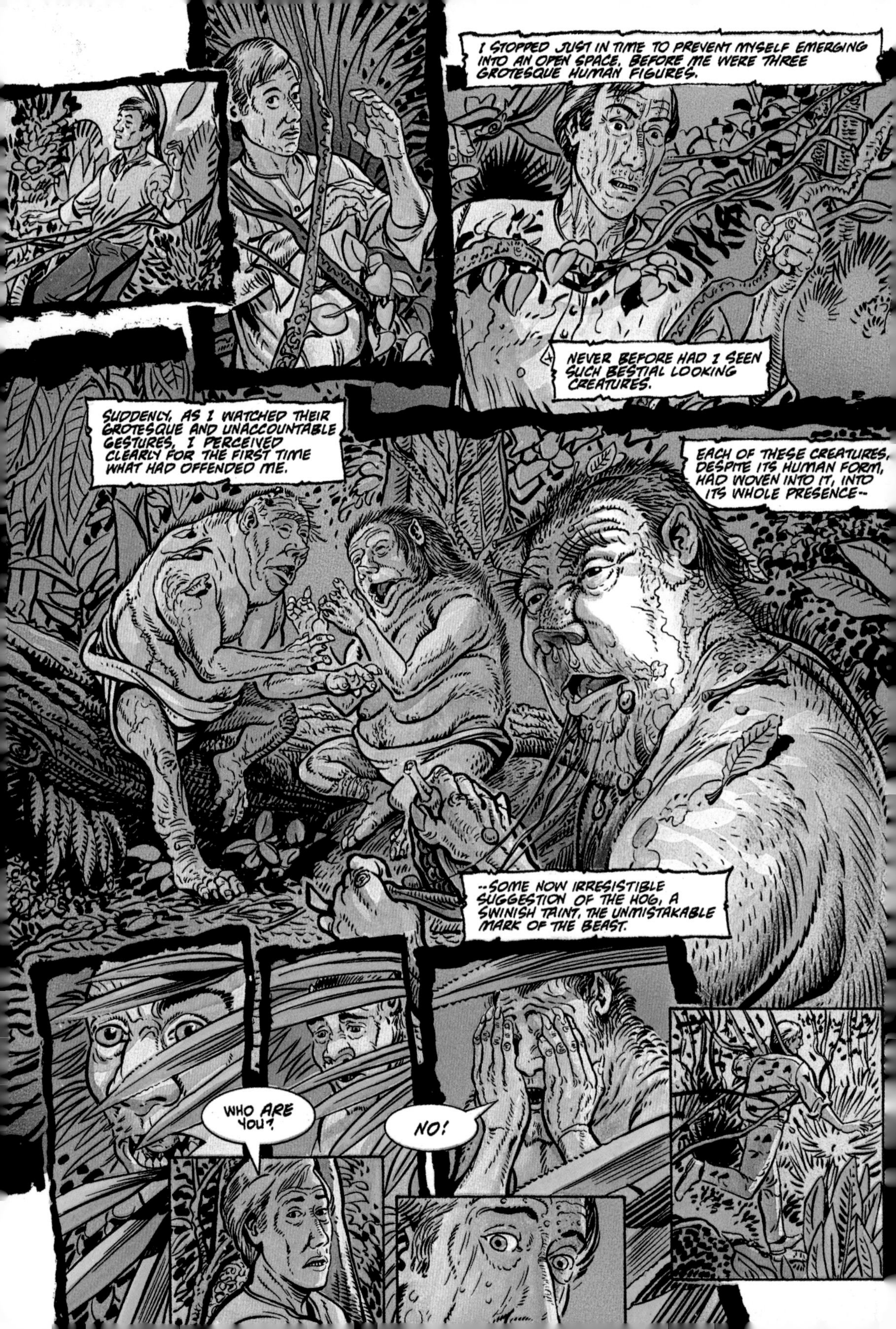
I STOPPED JUST IN TIME TO PREVENT MYSELF EMERGING INTO AN OPEN SPACE. BEFORE ME WERE THREE GROTESQUE HUMAN FIGURES.
NEVER BEFORE HAD I SEEN SUCH BESTIAL LOOKING CREATURES.
SUDDENLY, AS I WATCHED THEIR GROTESQUE AND UNACCOUNTABLE GESTURES, I PERCEIVED CLEARLY FOR THE FIRST TIME WHAT HAD OFFENDED ME.
EACH OF THESE CREATURES, DESPITE ITS HUMAN FORM, HAD WOVEN INTO IT, INTO ITS WHOLE PRESENCE--
--SOME NOW IRRESISTIBLE SUGGESTION OF THE HOG, A SWINISH TAINT, THE UNMISTAKABLE MARK OF THE BEAST.
WHO ARE YOU?
NO!

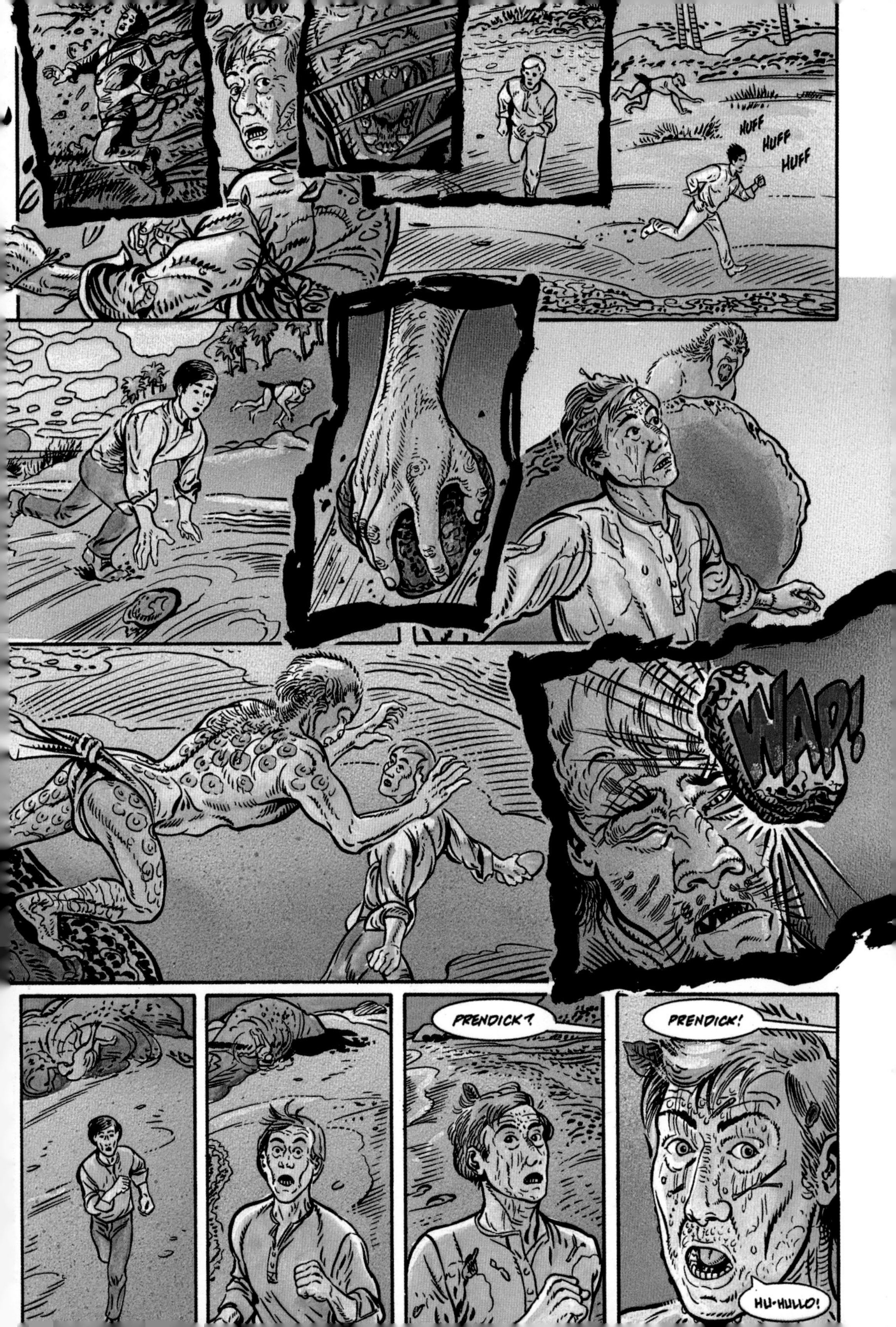
HUFF
HUFF
HUFF
WAP!
PRENDICK?
PRENDICK!
HU-HULLO!

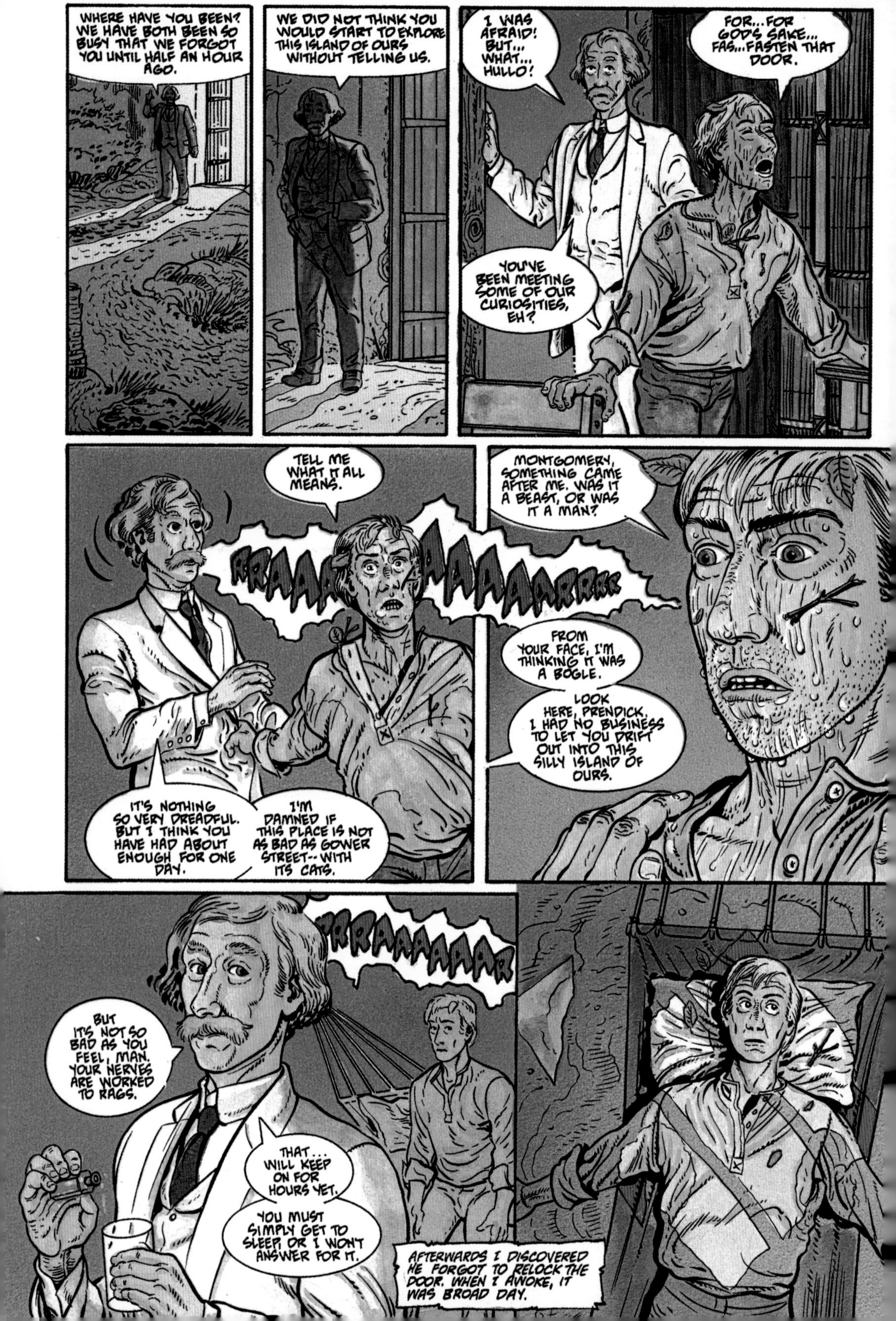
WHERE HAVE YOU BEEN? WE HAVE BOTH BEEN SO BUSY THAT WE FORGOT YOU UNTIL HALF AN HOUR AGO.
WE DID NOT THINK YOU WOULD START TO EXPLORE THIS ISLAND OF OURS WITHOUT TELLING US.
I WAS AFRAID! BUT... WHAT... HULLO!
FOR...FOR GOD'S SAKE... FAS...FASTEN THAT DOOR.
YOU'VE BEEN MEETING SOME OF OUR CURIOSITIES, EH?
TELL ME WHAT IT ALL MEANS.
RRAAAAAAAAAARRRRR
IT'S NOTHING SO VERY DREADFUL. BUT I THINK YOU HAVE HAD ABOUT ENOUGH FOR ONE DAY.
I'M DAMNED IF THIS PLACE IS NOT AS BAD AS GOWER STREET-- WITH ITS CATS.
MONTGOMERY, SOMETHING CAME AFTER ME. WAS IT A BEAST, OR WAS IT A MAN?
FROM YOUR FACE, I'M THINKING IT WAS A BOGLE.
LOOK HERE, PRENDICK, I HAD NO BUSINESS TO LET YOU DRIFT OUT INTO THIS SILLY ISLAND OF OURS.
RRRAAAAAAAR
BUT IT'S NOT SO BAD AS YOU FEEL, MAN. YOUR NERVES ARE WORKED TO RAGS.
THAT... WILL KEEP ON FOR HOURS YET.
YOU MUST SIMPLY GET TO SLEEP, OR I WON'T ANSWER FOR IT.
AFTERWARDS I DISCOVERED HE FORGOT TO RELOCK THE DOOR. WHEN I AWOKE, IT WAS BROAD DAY.

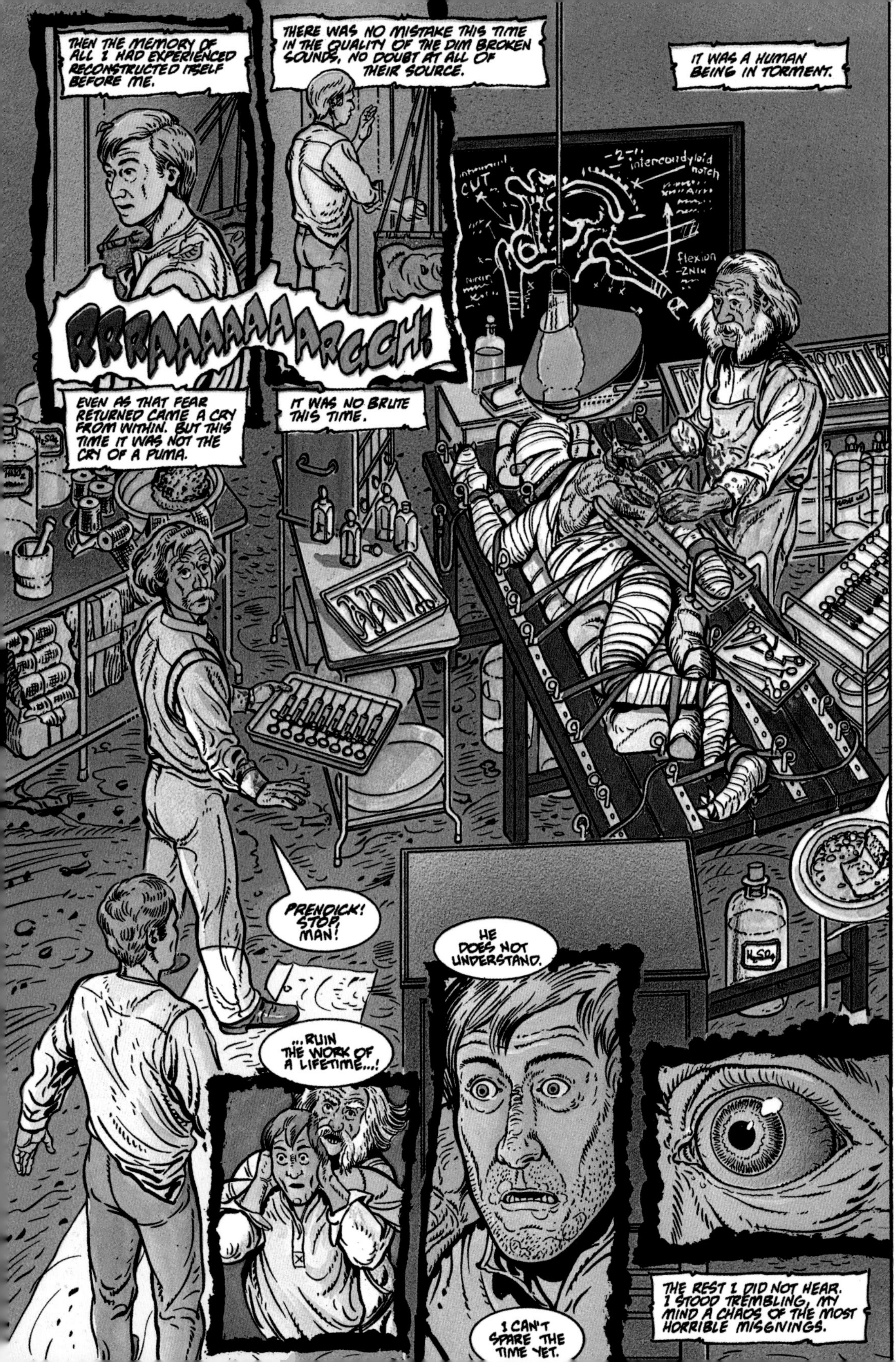
THEN THE MEMORY OF ALL I HAD EXPERIENCED RECONSTRUCTED ITSELF BEFORE ME.
THERE WAS NO MISTAKE THIS TIME IN THE QUALITY OF THE DIM BROKEN SOUNDS, NO DOUBT AT ALL OF THEIR SOURCE.
IT WAS A HUMAN BEING IN TORMENT.
RRRAAAAAAARGCH!
intercondyloid notch
CUT
flexion
EVEN AS THAT FEAR RETURNED CAME A CRY FROM WITHIN. BUT THIS TIME IT WAS NOT THE CRY OF A PUMA.
IT WAS NO BRUTE THIS TIME.
PRENDICK! STOP, MAN!
HE DOES NOT UNDERSTAND.
...RUIN THE WORK OF A LIFETIME...!
I CAN'T SPARE THE TIME YET.
THE REST I DID NOT HEAR. I STOOD TREMBLING, MY MIND A CHAOS OF THE MOST HORRIBLE MISGIVINGS.

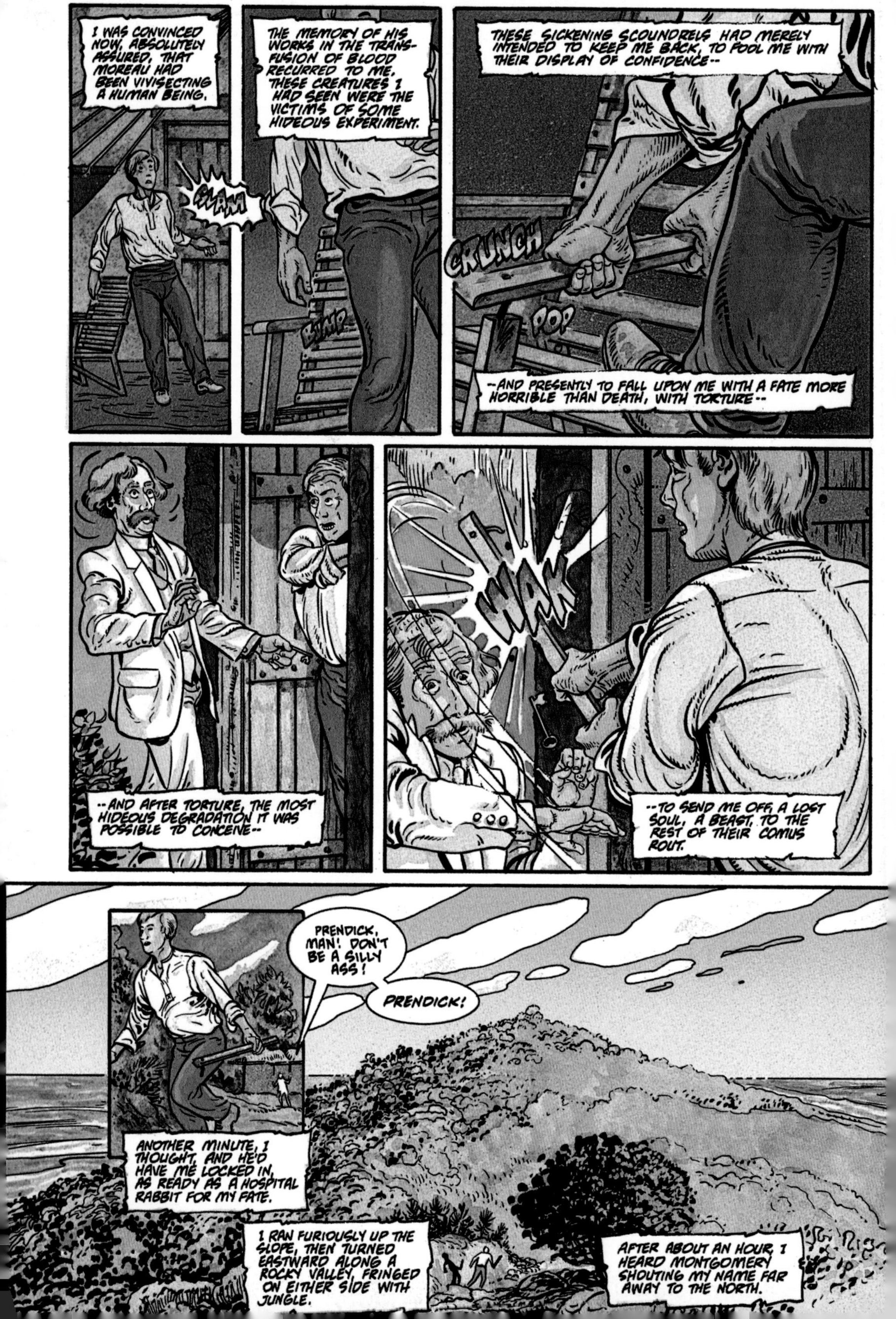
I WAS CONVINCED NOW, ABSOLUTELY ASSURED, THAT MOREAU HAD BEEN VIVISECTING A HUMAN BEING.
BLAM
THE MEMORY OF HIS WORKS IN THE TRANSFUSION OF BLOOD RECURRED TO ME. THESE CREATURES I HAD SEEN WERE THE VICTIMS OF SOME HIDEOUS EXPERIMENT.
BUMP
THESE SICKENING SCOUNDRELS HAD MERELY INTENDED TO KEEP ME BACK, TO FOOL ME WITH THEIR DISPLAY OF CONFIDENCE--
CRUNCH
POP
--AND PRESENTLY TO FALL UPON ME WITH A FATE MORE HORRIBLE THAN DEATH, WITH TORTURE--
--AND AFTER TORTURE, THE MOST HIDEOUS DEGRADATION IT WAS POSSIBLE TO CONCEIVE--
WAK
--TO SEND ME OFF, A LOST SOUL, A BEAST, TO THE REST OF THEIR COMUS ROUT.
ANOTHER MINUTE, I THOUGHT, AND HE'D HAVE ME LOCKED IN, AS READY AS A HOSPITAL RABBIT FOR MY FATE.
PRENDICK, MAN! DON'T BE A SILLY ASS!
PRENDICK!
I RAN FURIOUSLY UP THE SLOPE, THEN TURNED EASTWARD ALONG A ROCKY VALLEY, FRINGED ON EITHER SIDE WITH JUNGLE.
AFTER ABOUT AN HOUR, I HEARD MONTGOMERY SHOUTING MY NAME FAR AWAY TO THE NORTH.

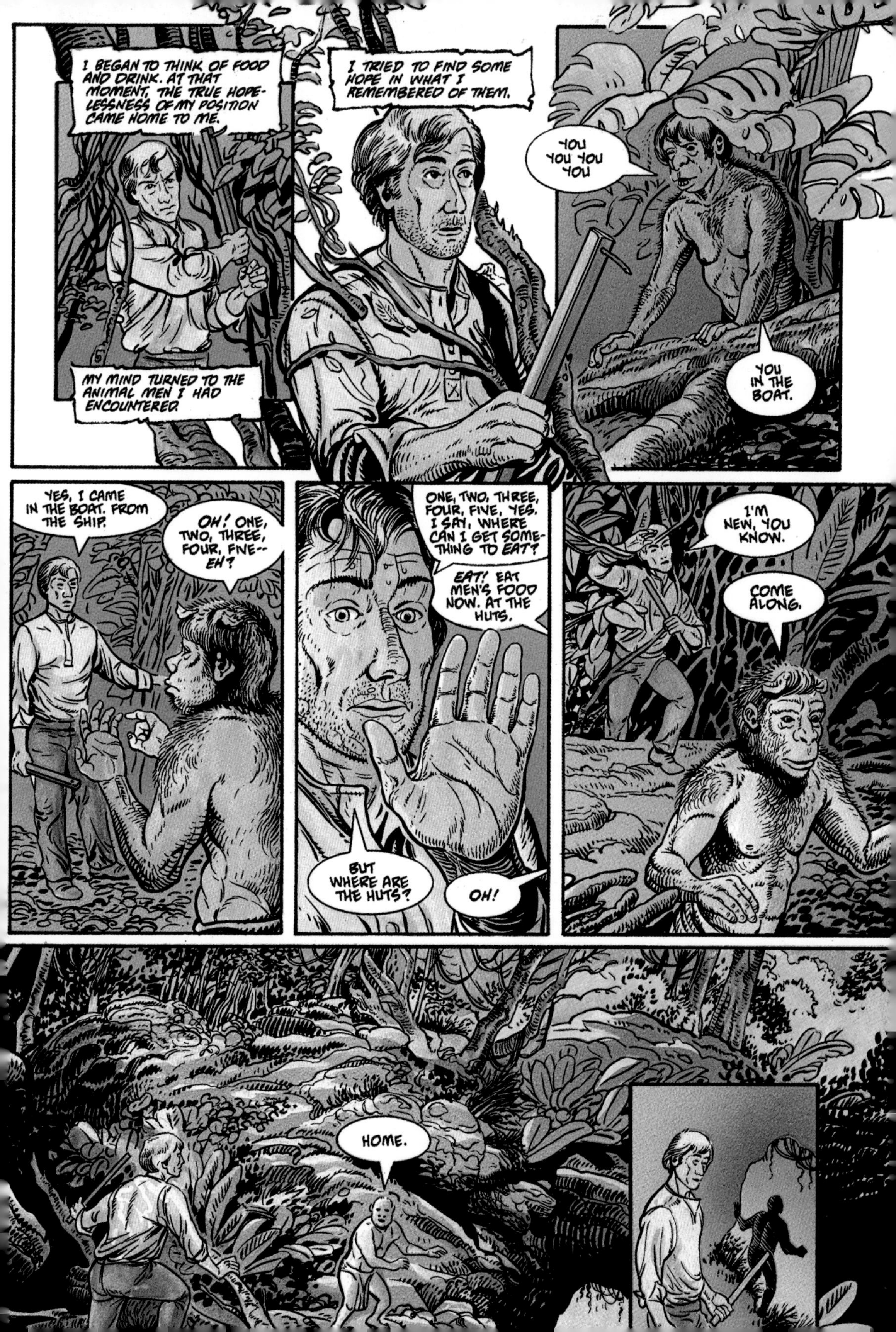
I BEGAN TO THINK OF FOOD AND DRINK. AT THAT MOMENT, THE TRUE HOPELESSNESS OF MY POSITION CAME HOME TO ME.
MY MIND TURNED TO THE ANIMAL MEN I HAD ENCOUNTERED.
I TRIED TO FIND SOME HOPE IN WHAT I REMEMBERED OF THEM.
YOU YOU YOU YOU
YOU IN THE BOAT.
YES, I CAME IN THE BOAT. FROM THE SHIP.
OH! ONE, TWO, THREE, FOUR, FIVE-- EH?
ONE, TWO, THREE, FOUR, FIVE, YES. I SAY, WHERE CAN I GET SOMETHING TO EAT?
EAT! EAT MEN'S FOOD NOW. AT THE HUTS.
BUT WHERE ARE THE HUTS?
OH!
I'M NEW, YOU KNOW.
COME ALONG.
HOME.

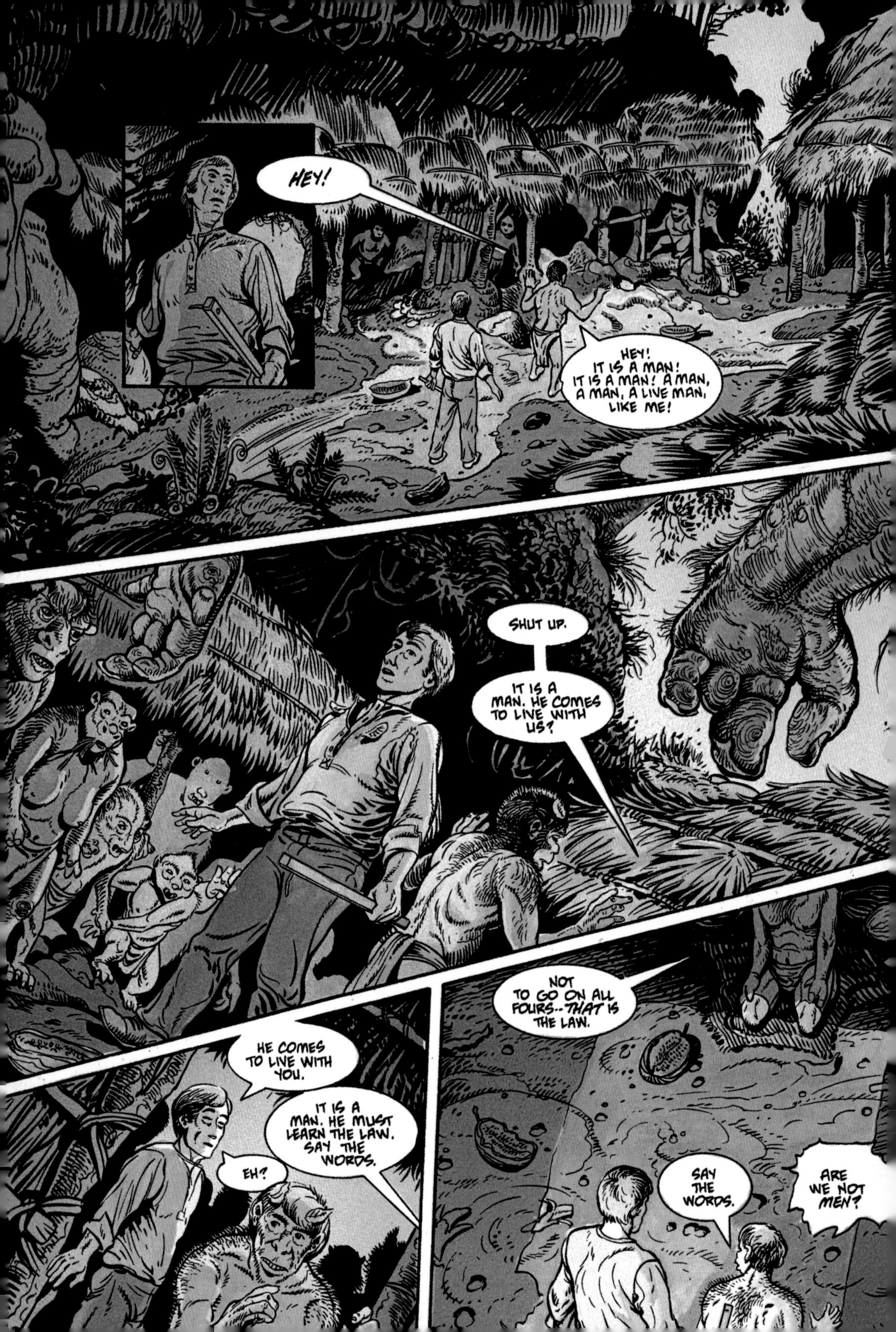

HEY!
HEY! IT IS A MAN! IT IS A MAN! A MAN, A MAN, A LIVE MAN, LIKE ME!
SHUT UP.
IT IS A MAN. HE COMES TO LIVE WITH US?
HE COMES TO LIVE WITH YOU.
IT IS A MAN. HE MUST LEARN THE LAW. SAY THE WORDS.
EH?
NOT TO GO ON ALL FOURS--THAT IS THE LAW.
SAY THE WORDS.
ARE WE NOT MEN?

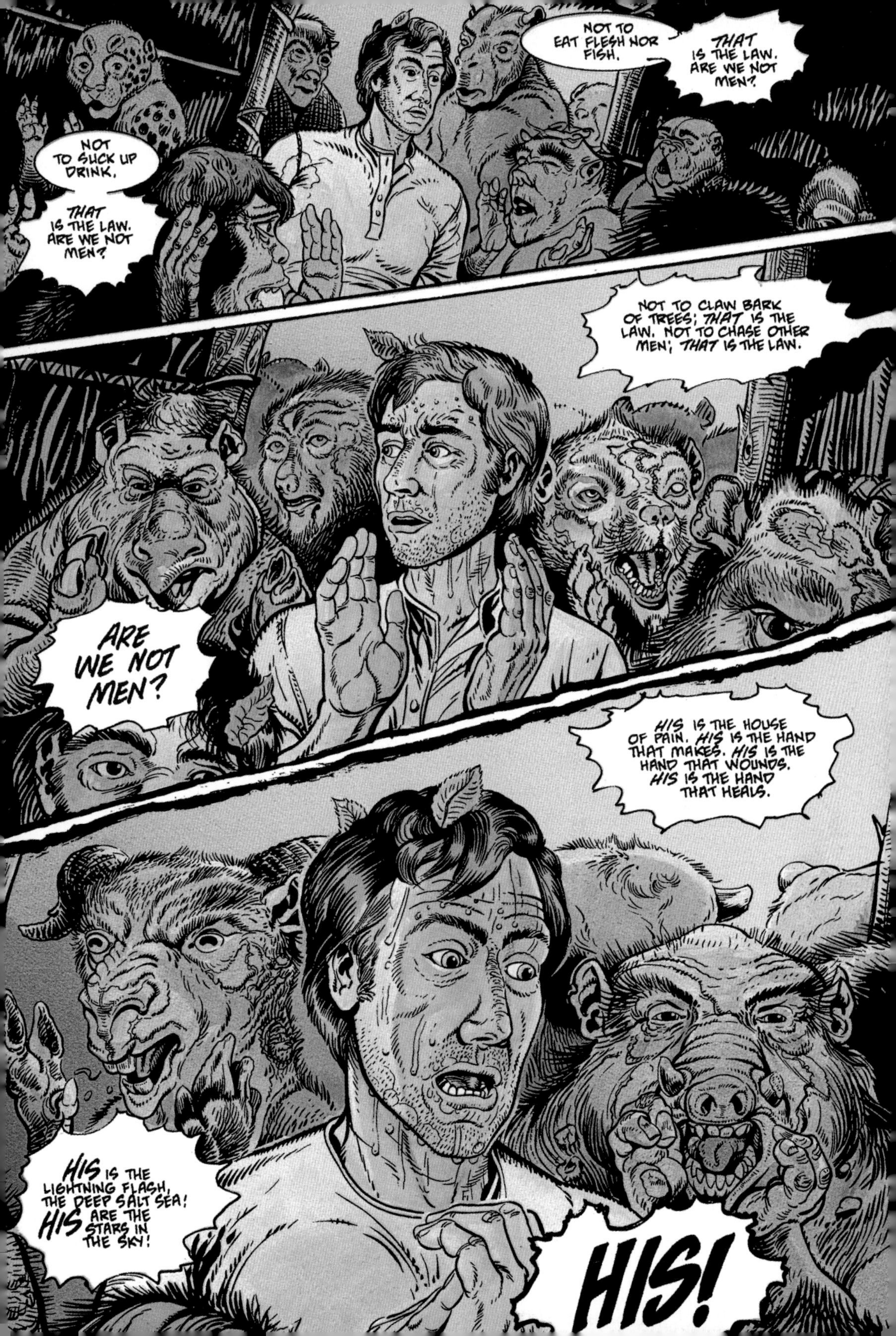
NOT TO EAT FLESH NOR FISH.
THAT IS THE LAW. ARE WE NOT MEN?
NOT TO SUCK UP DRINK.
THAT IS THE LAW. ARE WE NOT MEN?
NOT TO CLAW BARK OF TREES; THAT IS THE LAW. NOT TO CHASE OTHER MEN; THAT IS THE LAW.
ARE WE NOT MEN?
HIS IS THE HOUSE OF PAIN. HIS IS THE HAND THAT MAKES. HIS IS THE HAND THAT WOUNDS. HIS IS THE HAND THAT HEALS.
HIS IS THE LIGHTNING FLASH, THE DEEP SALT SEA! HIS ARE THE STARS IN THE SKY!
HIS!

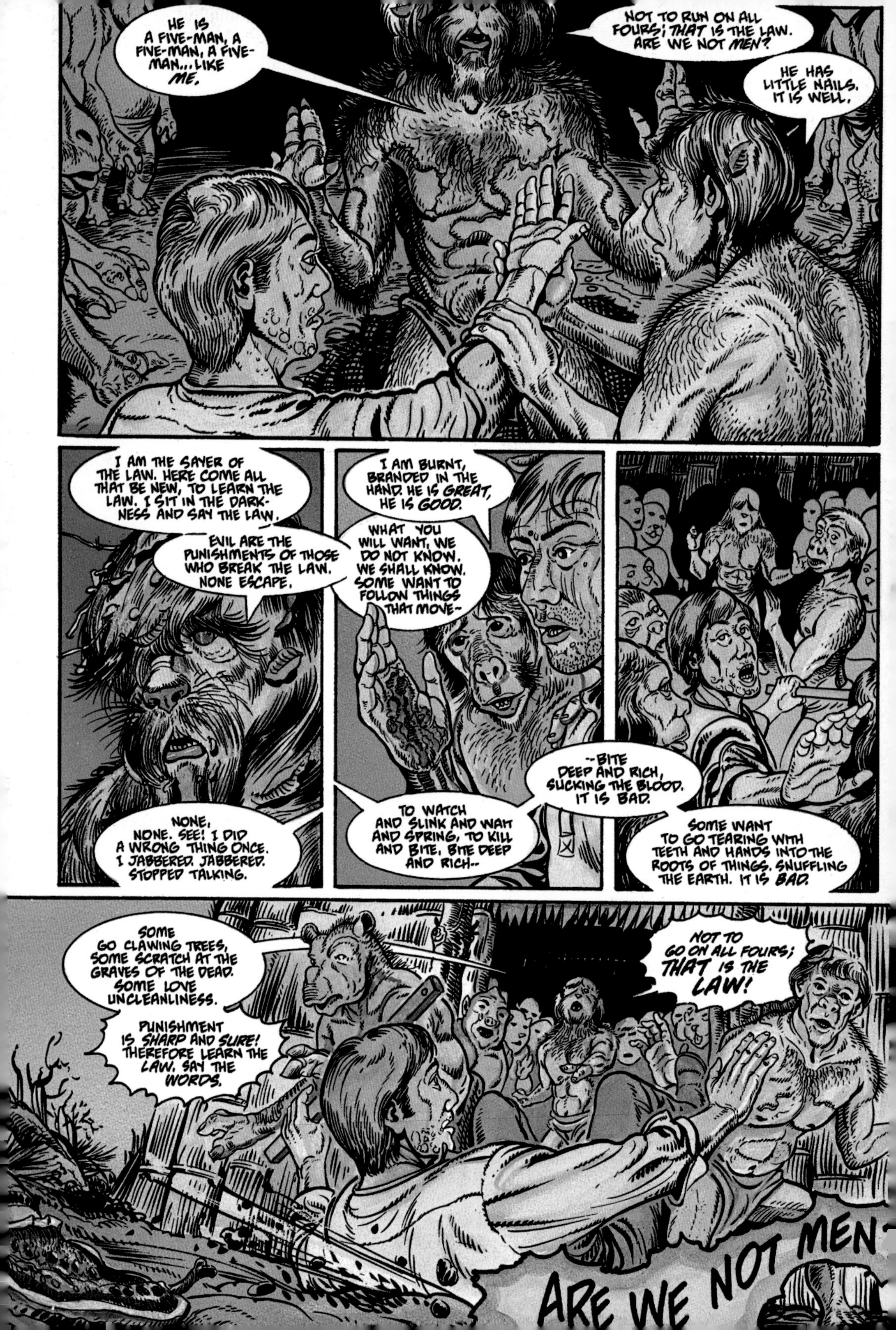
HE IS A FIVE-MAN, A FIVE-MAN, A FIVE-MAN... LIKE ME.
NOT TO RUN ON ALL FOURS; THAT IS THE LAW. ARE WE NOT MEN?
HE HAS LITTLE NAILS. IT IS WELL.
I AM THE SAYER OF THE LAW. HERE COME ALL THAT BE NEW, TO LEARN THE LAW. I SIT IN THE DARKNESS AND SAY THE LAW.
EVIL ARE THE PUNISHMENTS OF THOSE WHO BREAK THE LAW. NONE ESCAPE.
NONE, NONE. SEE! I DID A WRONG THING ONCE. I JABBERED. JABBERED. STOPPED TALKING.
I AM BURNT, BRANDED IN THE HAND. HE IS GREAT, HE IS GOOD.
WHAT YOU WILL WANT, WE DO NOT KNOW. WE SHALL KNOW. SOME WANT TO FOLLOW THINGS THAT MOVE-
TO WATCH AND SLINK AND WAIT AND SPRING, TO KILL AND BITE, BITE DEEP AND RICH--
--BITE DEEP AND RICH, SUCKING THE BLOOD. IT IS BAD.
SOME WANT TO GO TEARING WITH TEETH AND HANDS INTO THE ROOTS OF THINGS. SNUFFLING THE EARTH. IT IS BAD.
SOME GO CLAWING TREES, SOME SCRATCH AT THE GRAVES OF THE DEAD. SOME LOVE UNCLEANLINESS.
PUNISHMENT IS SHARP AND SURE! THEREFORE LEARN THE LAW. SAY THE WORDS.
NOT TO GO ON ALL FOURS; THAT IS THE LAW!
ARE WE NOT MEN-

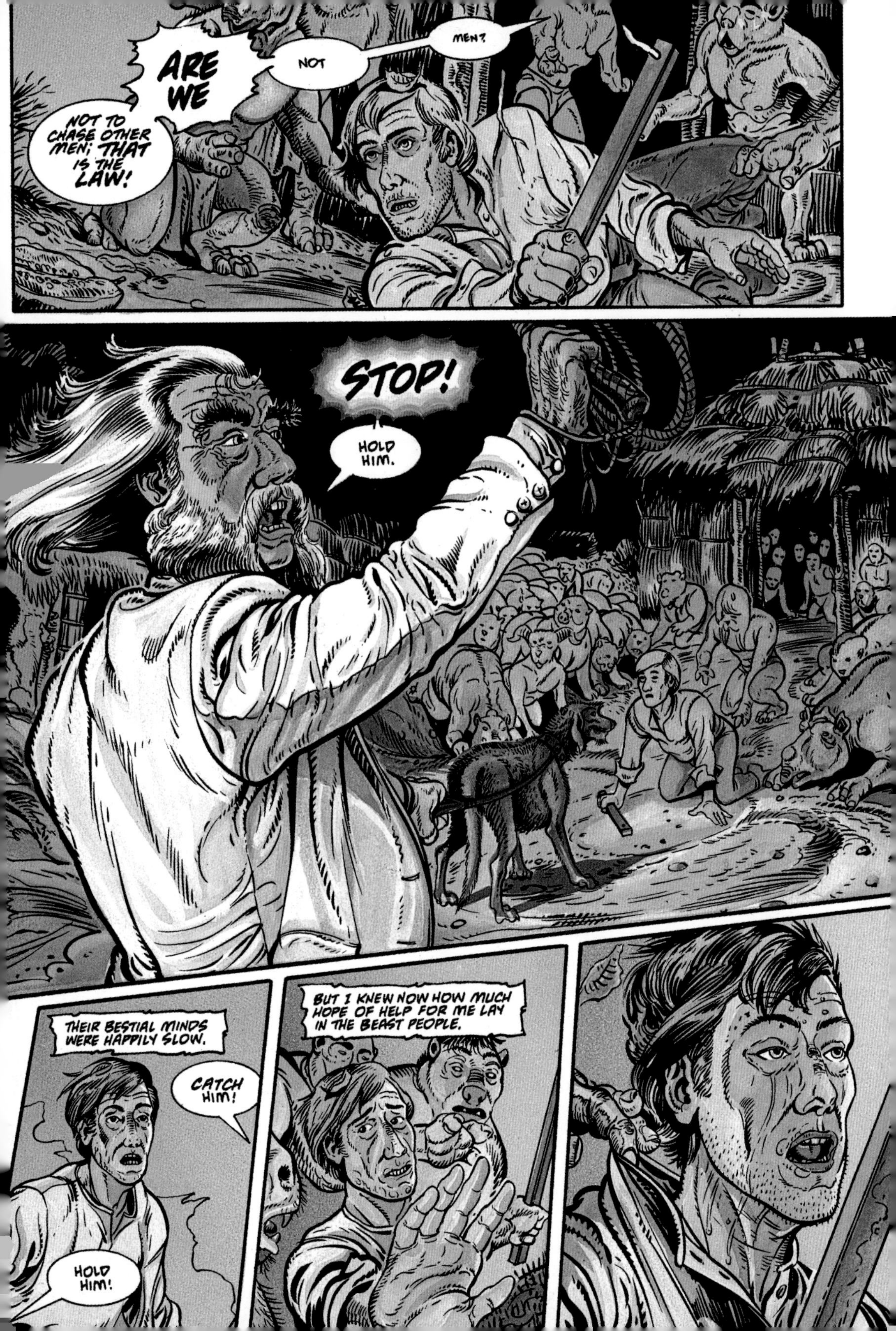
ARE WE
NOT
MEN?
NOT TO CHASE OTHER MEN; THAT IS THE LAW!
STOP!
HOLD HIM.
THEIR BESTIAL MINDS WERE HAPPILY SLOW.
CATCH HIM!
HOLD HIM!
BUT I KNEW NOW HOW MUCH HOPE OF HELP FOR ME LAY IN THE BEAST PEOPLE.

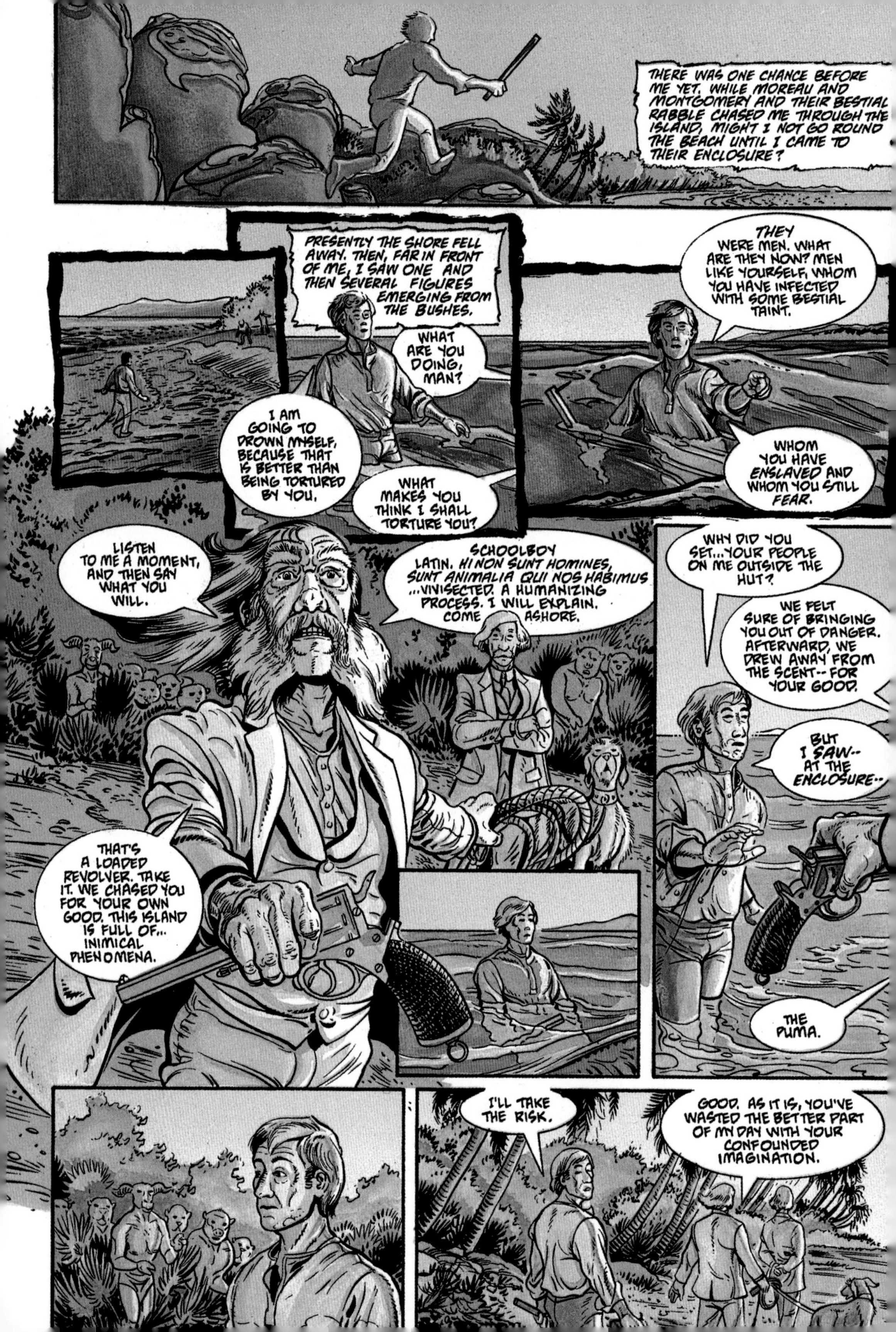

THERE WAS ONE CHANCE BEFORE ME YET. WHILE MOREAU AND MONTGOMERY AND THEIR BESTIAL RABBLE CHASED ME THROUGH THE ISLAND, MIGHT I NOT GO ROUND THE BEACH UNTIL I CAME TO THEIR ENCLOSURE?
PRESENTLY THE SHORE FELL AWAY. THEN, FAR IN FRONT OF ME, I SAW ONE AND THEN SEVERAL FIGURES EMERGING FROM THE BUSHES.
WHAT ARE YOU DOING, MAN?
I AM GOING TO DROWN MYSELF, BECAUSE THAT IS BETTER THAN BEING TORTURED BY YOU.
WHAT MAKES YOU THINK I SHALL TORTURE YOU?
THEY WERE MEN. WHAT ARE THEY NOW? MEN LIKE YOURSELF, WHOM YOU HAVE INFECTED WITH SOME BESTIAL TAINT.
WHOM YOU HAVE ENSLAVED AND WHOM YOU STILL FEAR.
LISTEN TO ME A MOMENT, AND THEN SAY WHAT YOU WILL.
SCHOOLBOY LATIN. HI NON SUNT HOMINES, SUNT ANIMALIA QUI NOS HABIMUS ...VIVISECTED. A HUMANIZING PROCESS. I WILL EXPLAIN. COME ASHORE.
THAT'S A LOADED REVOLVER. TAKE IT. WE CHASED YOU FOR YOUR OWN GOOD. THIS ISLAND IS FULL OF... INIMICAL PHENOMENA.
WHY DID YOU SET...YOUR PEOPLE ON ME OUTSIDE THE HUT?
WE FELT SURE OF BRINGING YOU OUT OF DANGER. AFTERWARD, WE DREW AWAY FROM THE SCENT-- FOR YOUR GOOD.
BUT I SAW-- AT THE ENCLOSURE--
THE PUMA.
I'LL TAKE THE RISK.
GOOD. AS IT IS, YOU'VE WASTED THE BETTER PART OF MY DAY WITH YOUR CONFOUNDED IMAGINATION.

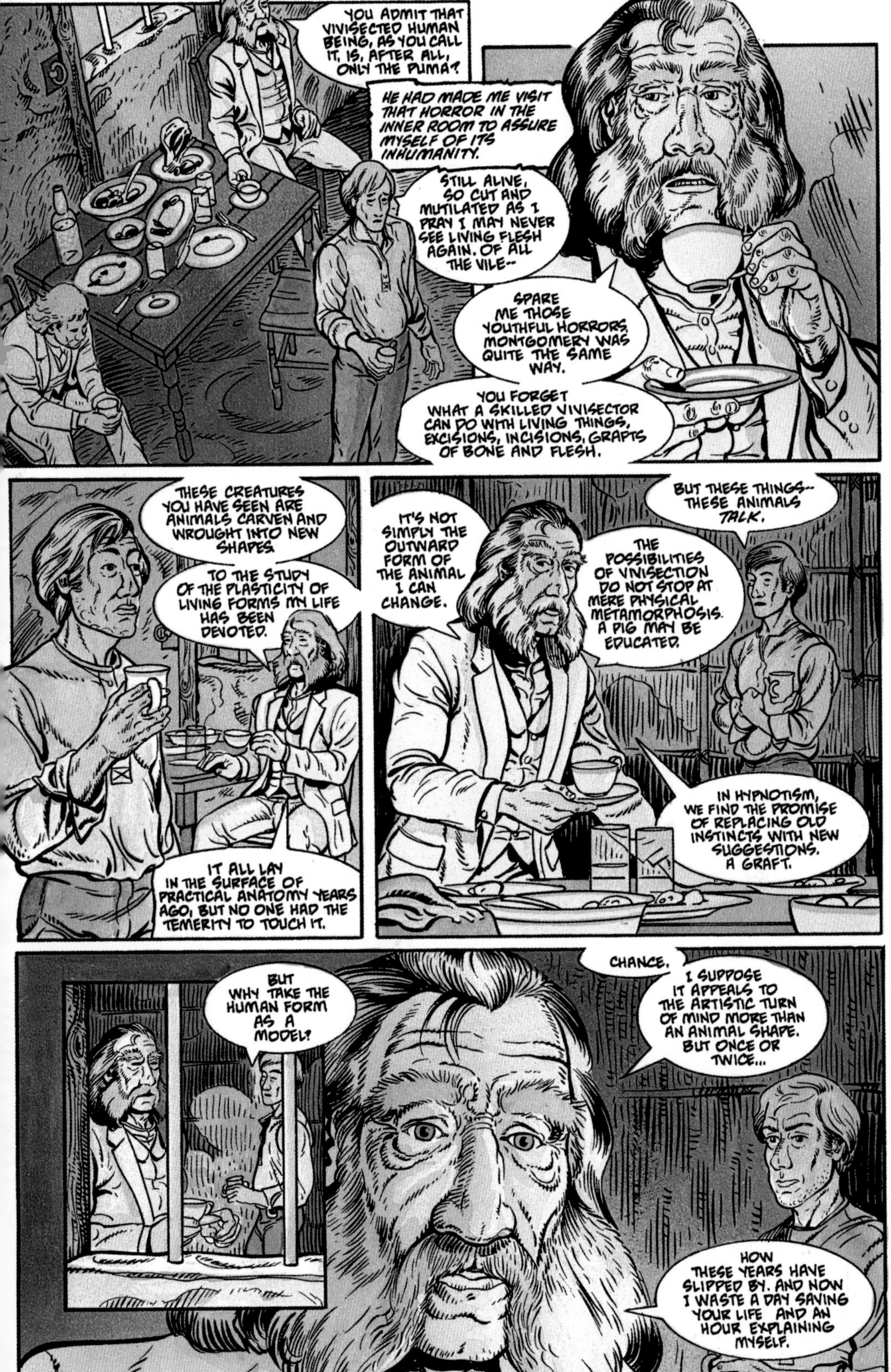
YOU ADMIT THAT VIVISECTED HUMAN BEING, AS YOU CALL IT, IS, AFTER ALL, ONLY THE PUMA?
HE HAD MADE ME VISIT THAT HORROR IN THE INNER ROOM TO ASSURE MYSELF OF ITS INHUMANITY.
STILL ALIVE, SO CUT AND MUTILATED AS I PRAY I MAY NEVER SEE LIVING FLESH AGAIN. OF ALL THE VILE--
SPARE ME THOSE YOUTHFUL HORRORS. MONTGOMERY WAS QUITE THE SAME WAY.
YOU FORGET WHAT A SKILLED VIVISECTOR CAN DO WITH LIVING THINGS, EXCISIONS, INCISIONS, GRAFTS OF BONE AND FLESH.
THESE CREATURES YOU HAVE SEEN ARE ANIMALS CARVEN AND WROUGHT INTO NEW SHAPES.
TO THE STUDY OF THE PLASTICITY OF LIVING FORMS MY LIFE HAS BEEN DEVOTED.
IT ALL LAY IN THE SURFACE OF PRACTICAL ANATOMY YEARS AGO, BUT NO ONE HAD THE TEMERITY TO TOUCH IT.
IT'S NOT SIMPLY THE OUTWARD FORM OF THE ANIMAL I CAN CHANGE.
BUT THESE THINGS-- THESE ANIMALS TALK.
THE POSSIBILITIES OF VIVISECTION DO NOT STOP AT MERE PHYSICAL METAMORPHOSIS. A PIG MAY BE EDUCATED.
IN HYPNOTISM, WE FIND THE PROMISE OF REPLACING OLD INSTINCTS WITH NEW SUGGESTIONS. A GRAFT.
BUT WHY TAKE THE HUMAN FORM AS A MODEL?
CHANCE.
I SUPPOSE IT APPEALS TO THE ARTISTIC TURN OF MIND MORE THAN AN ANIMAL SHAPE. BUT ONCE OR TWICE...
HOW THESE YEARS HAVE SLIPPED BY. AND NOW I WASTE A DAY SAVING YOUR LIFE AND AN HOUR EXPLAINING MYSELF.

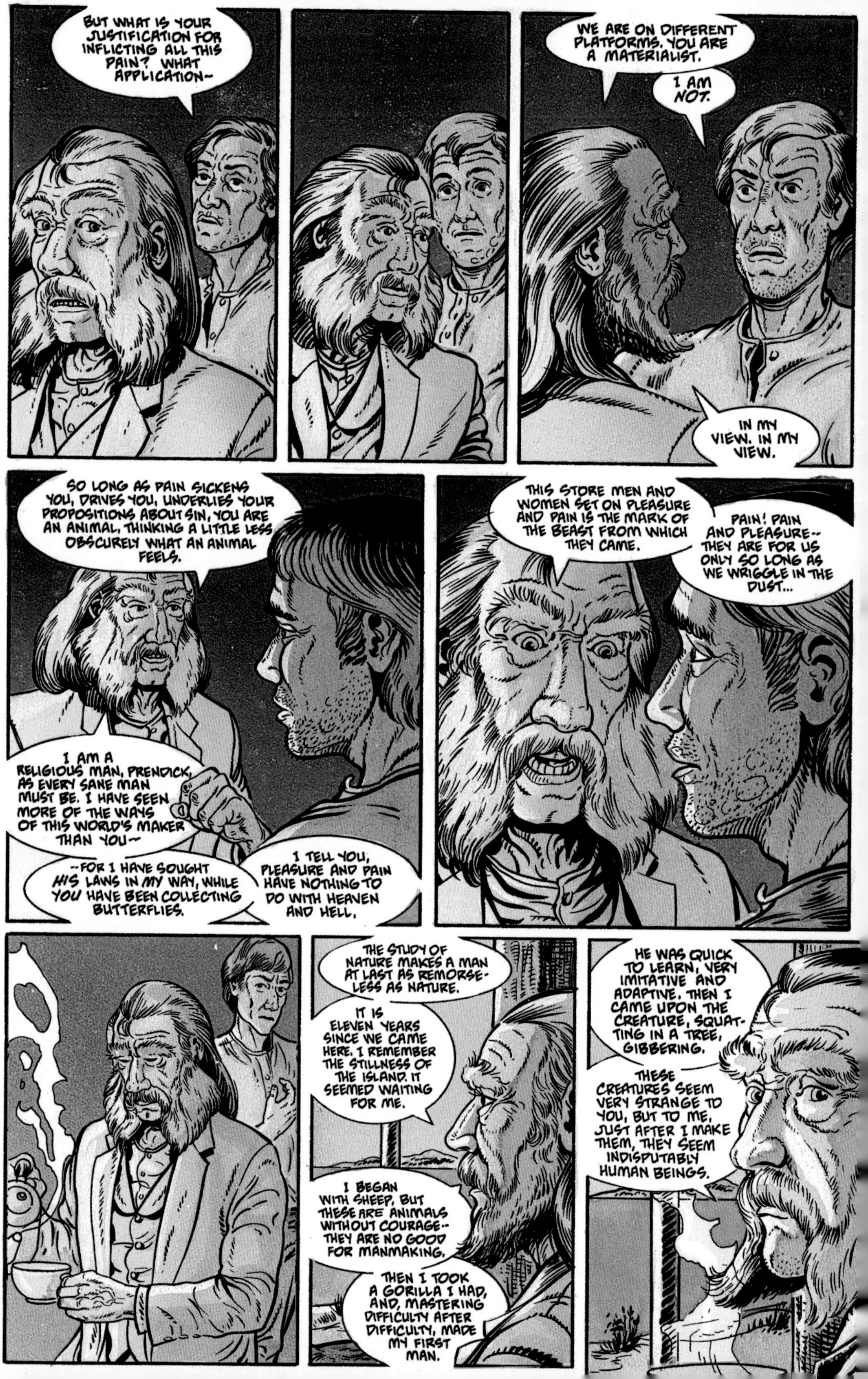

BUT WHAT IS YOUR JUSTIFICATION FOR INFLICTING ALL THIS PAIN? WHAT APPLICATION--
WE ARE ON DIFFERENT PLATFORMS. YOU ARE A MATERIALIST.
I AM *NOT*.
IN MY VIEW. IN MY VIEW.
SO LONG AS PAIN SICKENS YOU, DRIVES YOU, UNDERLIES YOUR PROPOSITIONS ABOUT SIN, YOU ARE AN ANIMAL, THINKING A LITTLE LESS OBSCURELY WHAT AN ANIMAL FEELS.
I AM A RELIGIOUS MAN, PRENDICK, AS EVERY SANE MAN MUST BE. I HAVE SEEN MORE OF THE WAYS OF THIS WORLD'S MAKER THAN YOU--
--FOR I HAVE SOUGHT *HIS* LAWS IN *MY* WAY, WHILE *YOU* HAVE BEEN COLLECTING BUTTERFLIES.
I TELL YOU, PLEASURE AND PAIN HAVE NOTHING TO DO WITH HEAVEN AND HELL.
THIS STORE MEN AND WOMEN SET ON PLEASURE AND PAIN IS THE MARK OF THE BEAST FROM WHICH THEY CAME.
PAIN! PAIN AND PLEASURE-- THEY ARE FOR US ONLY SO LONG AS WE WRIGGLE IN THE DUST...
THE STUDY OF NATURE MAKES A MAN AT LAST AS REMORSELESS AS NATURE.
IT IS ELEVEN YEARS SINCE WE CAME HERE. I REMEMBER THE STILLNESS OF THE ISLAND. IT SEEMED WAITING FOR ME.
I BEGAN WITH SHEEP, BUT THESE ARE ANIMALS WITHOUT COURAGE-- THEY ARE NO GOOD FOR MANMAKING.
THEN I TOOK A GORILLA I HAD, AND, MASTERING DIFFICULTY AFTER DIFFICULTY, MADE MY FIRST MAN.
HE WAS QUICK TO LEARN, VERY IMITATIVE AND ADAPTIVE. THEN I CAME UPON THE CREATURE, SQUATTING IN A TREE, GIBBERING.
THESE CREATURES SEEM VERY STRANGE TO YOU, BUT TO ME, JUST AFTER I MAKE THEM, THEY SEEM INDISPUTABLY HUMAN BEINGS.

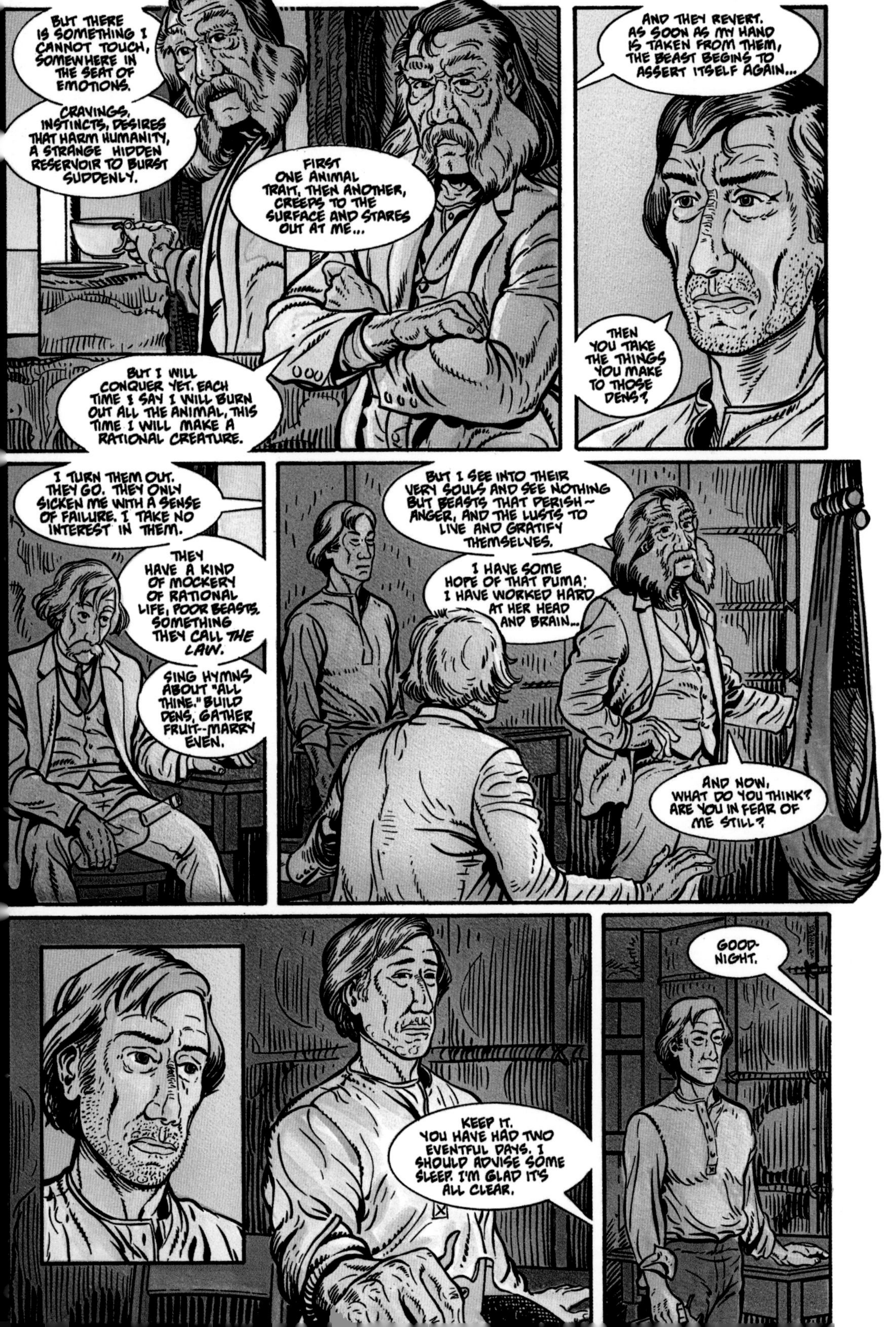
BUT THERE IS SOMETHING I CANNOT TOUCH, SOMEWHERE IN THE SEAT OF EMOTIONS.
CRAVINGS, INSTINCTS, DESIRES THAT HARM HUMANITY, A STRANGE HIDDEN RESERVOIR TO BURST SUDDENLY.
FIRST ONE ANIMAL TRAIT, THEN ANOTHER, CREEPS TO THE SURFACE AND STARES OUT AT ME...
BUT I WILL CONQUER YET. EACH TIME I SAY I WILL BURN OUT ALL THE ANIMAL, THIS TIME I WILL MAKE A RATIONAL CREATURE.
AND THEY REVERT. AS SOON AS MY HAND IS TAKEN FROM THEM, THE BEAST BEGINS TO ASSERT ITSELF AGAIN...
THEN YOU TAKE THE THINGS YOU MAKE TO THOSE DENS?
I TURN THEM OUT. THEY GO. THEY ONLY SICKEN ME WITH A SENSE OF FAILURE. I TAKE NO INTEREST IN THEM.
THEY HAVE A KIND OF MOCKERY OF RATIONAL LIFE, POOR BEASTS. SOMETHING THEY CALL THE LAW.
SING HYMNS ABOUT "ALL THINE." BUILD DENS, GATHER FRUIT--MARRY EVEN.
BUT I SEE INTO THEIR VERY SOULS AND SEE NOTHING BUT BEASTS THAT PERISH~ ANGER, AND THE LUSTS TO LIVE AND GRATIFY THEMSELVES.
I HAVE SOME HOPE OF THAT PUMA; I HAVE WORKED HARD AT HER HEAD AND BRAIN...
AND NOW, WHAT DO YOU THINK? ARE YOU IN FEAR OF ME STILL?
KEEP IT. YOU HAVE HAD TWO EVENTFUL DAYS. I SHOULD ADVISE SOME SLEEP. I'M GLAD IT'S ALL CLEAR.
GOOD-NIGHT.

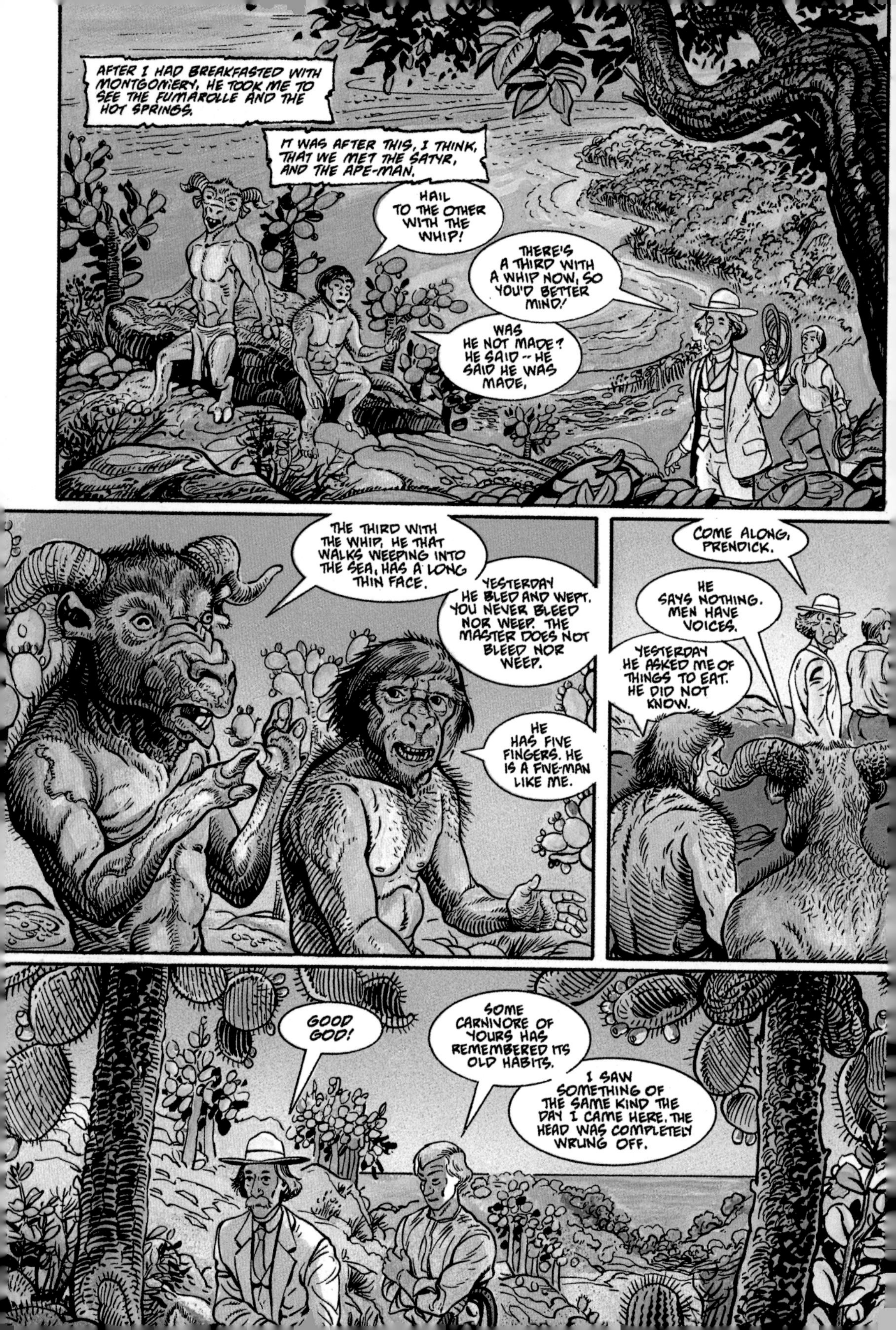
AFTER I HAD BREAKFASTED WITH MONTGOMERY, HE TOOK ME TO SEE THE FUMAROLLE AND THE HOT SPRINGS.
IT WAS AFTER THIS, I THINK, THAT WE MET THE SATYR, AND THE APE-MAN.
HAIL TO THE OTHER WITH THE WHIP!
THERE'S A THIRD WITH A WHIP NOW, SO YOU'D BETTER MIND!
WAS HE NOT MADE? HE SAID -- HE SAID HE WAS MADE.
THE THIRD WITH THE WHIP, HE THAT WALKS WEEPING INTO THE SEA, HAS A LONG THIN FACE.
YESTERDAY HE BLED AND WEPT. YOU NEVER BLEED NOR WEEP. THE MASTER DOES NOT BLEED NOR WEEP.
HE HAS FIVE FINGERS. HE IS A FIVE-MAN LIKE ME.
COME ALONG, PRENDICK.
HE SAYS NOTHING. MEN HAVE VOICES.
YESTERDAY HE ASKED ME OF THINGS TO EAT. HE DID NOT KNOW.
GOOD GOD!
SOME CARNIVORE OF YOURS HAS REMEMBERED ITS OLD HABITS.
I SAW SOMETHING OF THE SAME KIND THE DAY I CAME HERE. THE HEAD WAS COMPLETELY WRUNG OFF.

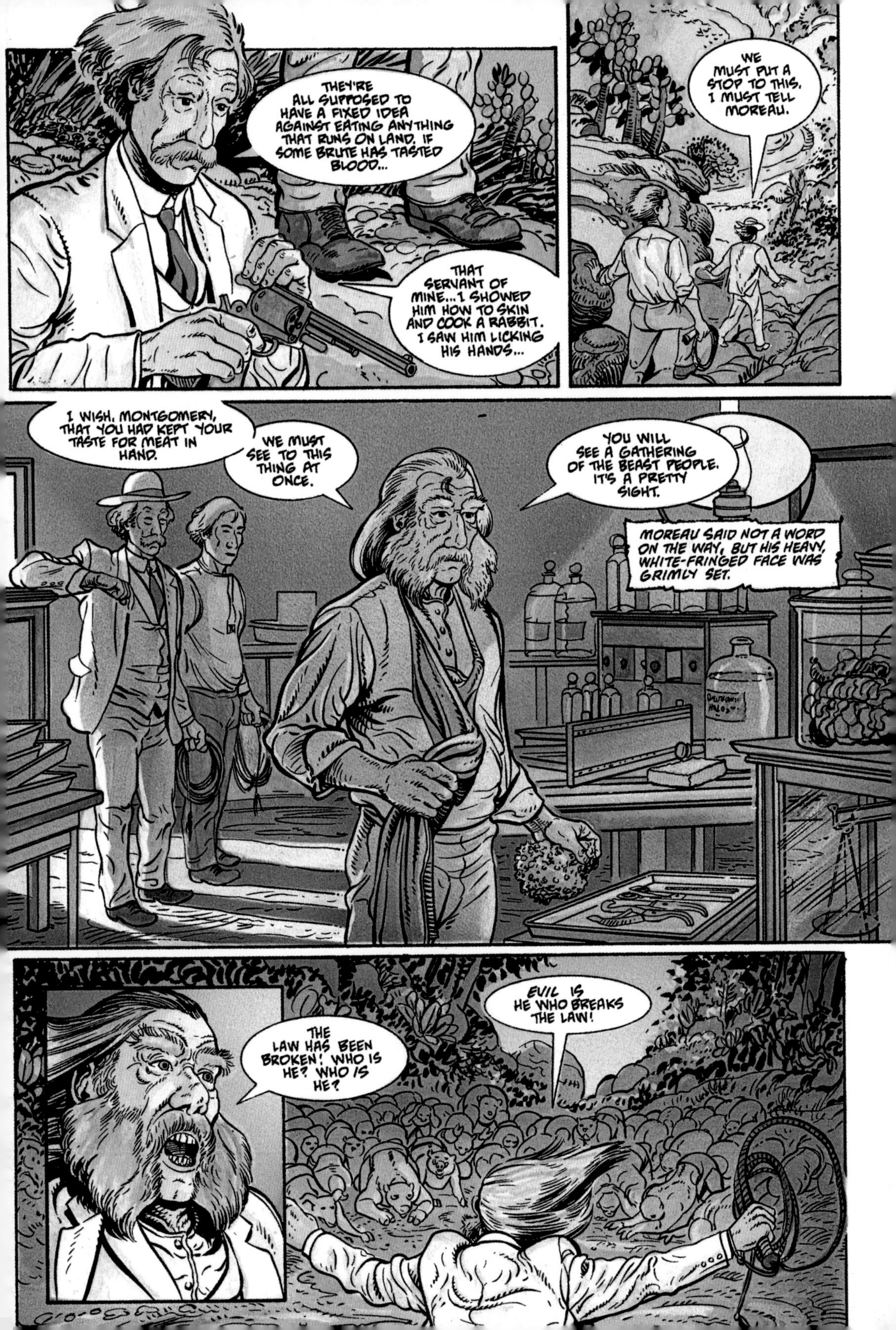
THEY'RE ALL SUPPOSED TO HAVE A FIXED IDEA AGAINST EATING ANYTHING THAT RUNS ON LAND. IF SOME BRUTE HAS TASTED BLOOD...
THAT SERVANT OF MINE...I SHOWED HIM HOW TO SKIN AND COOK A RABBIT. I SAW HIM LICKING HIS HANDS...
WE MUST PUT A STOP TO THIS. I MUST TELL MOREAU.
I WISH, MONTGOMERY, THAT YOU HAD KEPT YOUR TASTE FOR MEAT IN HAND.
WE MUST SEE TO THIS THING AT ONCE.
YOU WILL SEE A GATHERING OF THE BEAST PEOPLE. IT'S A PRETTY SIGHT.
MOREAU SAID NOT A WORD ON THE WAY, BUT HIS HEAVY, WHITE-FRINGED FACE WAS GRIMLY SET.
THE LAW HAS BEEN BROKEN! WHO IS HE? WHO IS HE?
EVIL IS HE WHO BREAKS THE LAW!

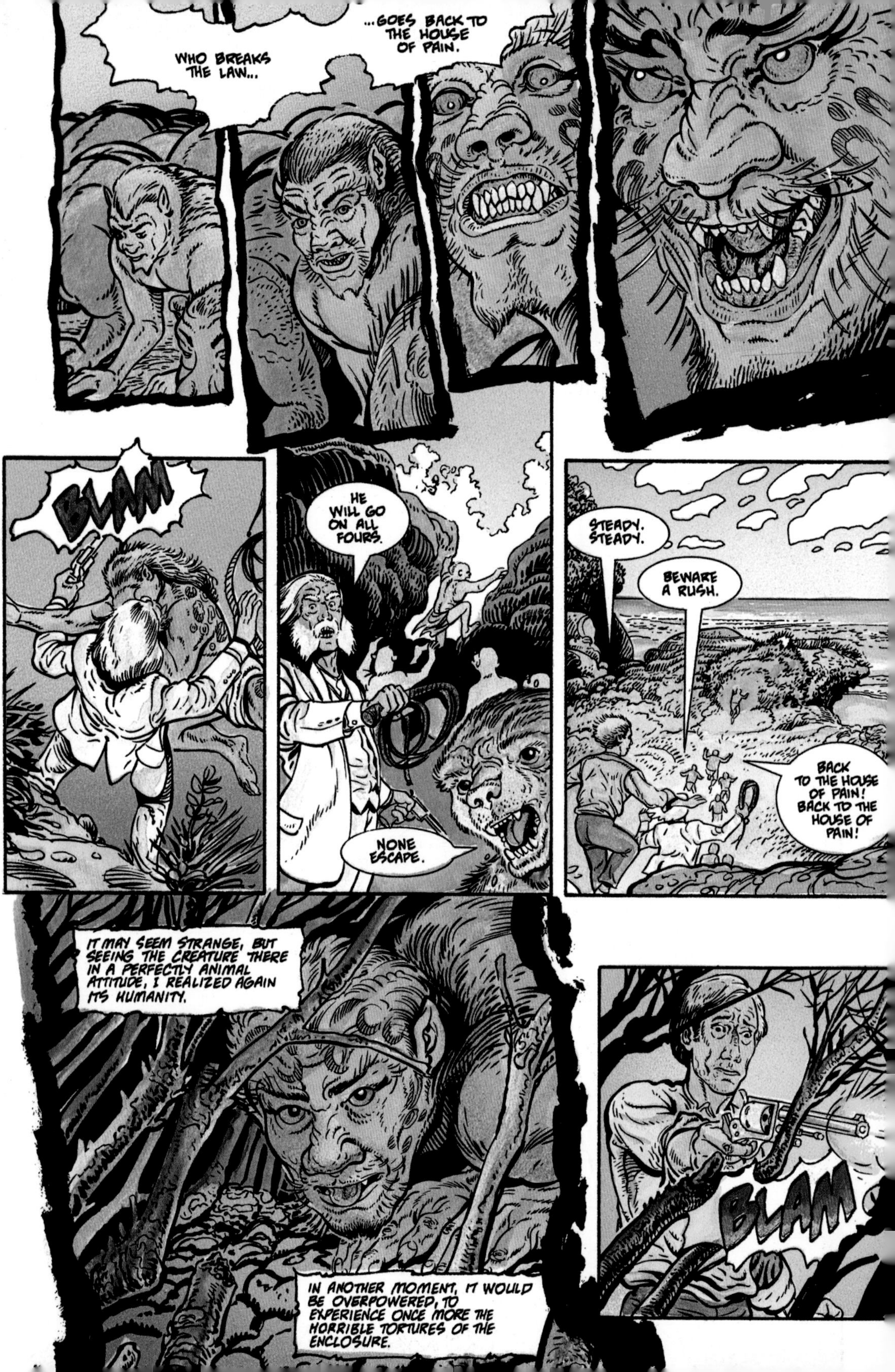
WHO BREAKS THE LAW...
...GOES BACK TO THE HOUSE OF PAIN.
BLAM
HE WILL GO ON ALL FOURS.
NONE ESCAPE.
STEADY. STEADY.
BEWARE A RUSH.
BACK TO THE HOUSE OF PAIN! BACK TO THE HOUSE OF PAIN!
IT MAY SEEM STRANGE, BUT SEEING THE CREATURE THERE IN A PERFECTLY ANIMAL ATTITUDE, I REALIZED AGAIN ITS HUMANITY.
IN ANOTHER MOMENT, IT WOULD BE OVERPOWERED, TO EXPERIENCE ONCE MORE THE HORRIBLE TORTURES OF THE ENCLOSURE.
BLAM

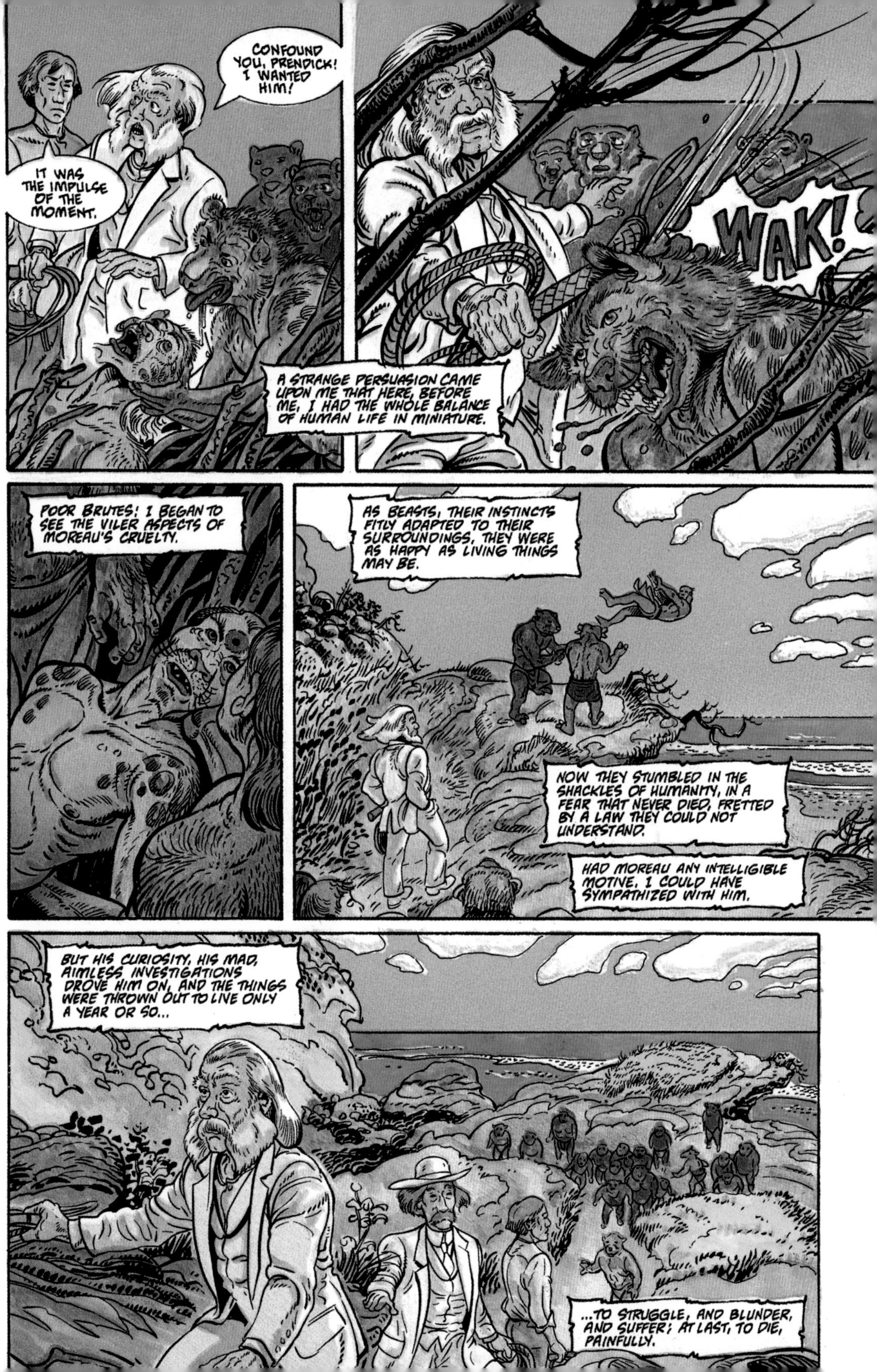
CONFOUND YOU, PRENDICK! I WANTED HIM!
IT WAS THE IMPULSE OF THE MOMENT.
A STRANGE PERSUASION CAME UPON ME THAT HERE, BEFORE ME, I HAD THE WHOLE BALANCE OF HUMAN LIFE IN MINIATURE.
WAK!
POOR BRUTES! I BEGAN TO SEE THE VILER ASPECTS OF MOREAU'S CRUELTY.
AS BEASTS, THEIR INSTINCTS FITLY ADAPTED TO THEIR SURROUNDINGS, THEY WERE AS HAPPY AS LIVING THINGS MAY BE.
NOW THEY STUMBLED IN THE SHACKLES OF HUMANITY, IN A FEAR THAT NEVER DIED, FRETTED BY A LAW THEY COULD NOT UNDERSTAND.
HAD MOREAU ANY INTELLIGIBLE MOTIVE, I COULD HAVE SYMPATHIZED WITH HIM.
BUT HIS CURIOSITY, HIS MAD, AIMLESS INVESTIGATIONS DROVE HIM ON, AND THE THINGS WERE THROWN OUT TO LIVE ONLY A YEAR OR SO...
...TO STRUGGLE, AND BLUNDER, AND SUFFER; AT LAST, TO DIE, PAINFULLY.

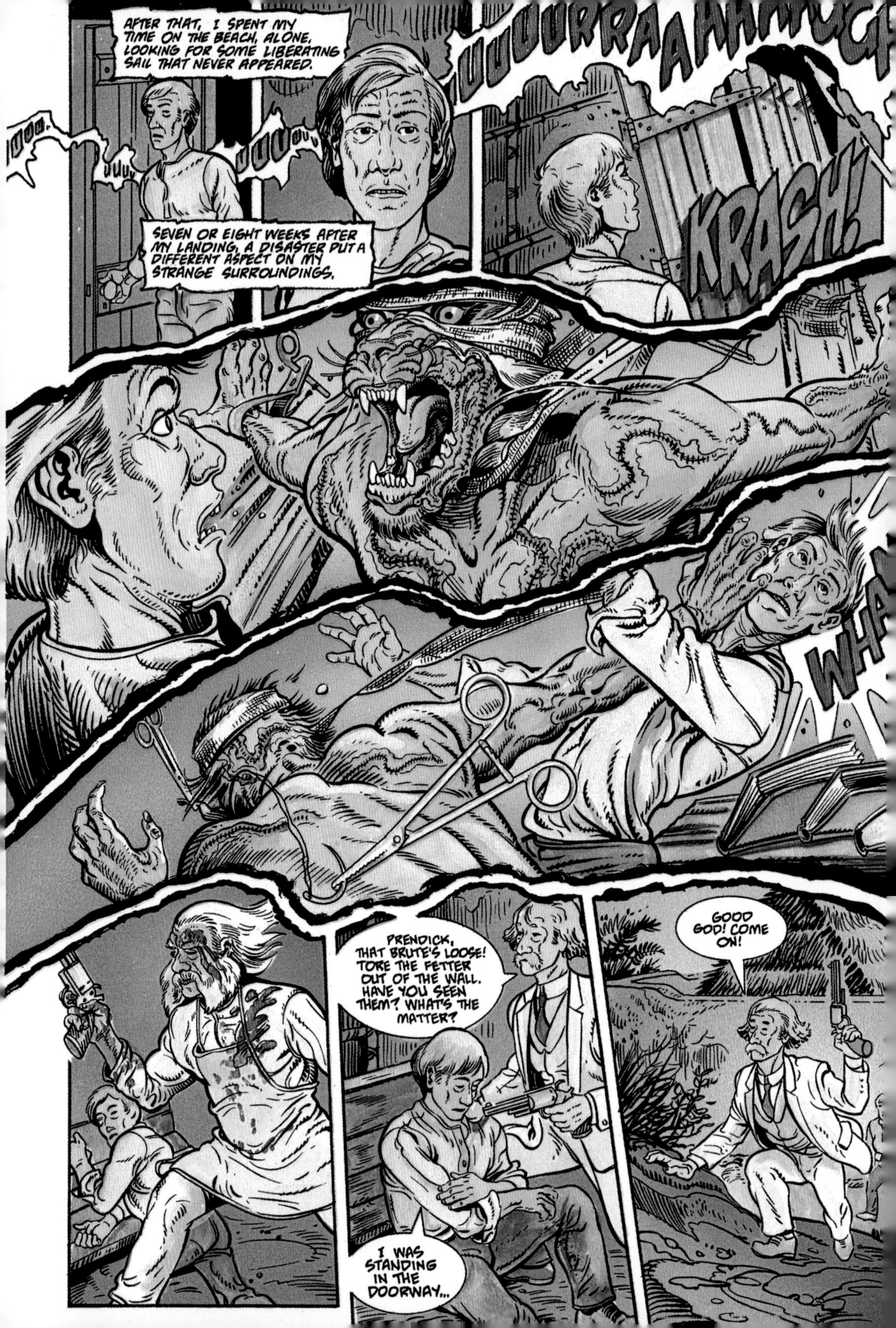
AFTER THAT, I SPENT MY TIME ON THE BEACH, ALONE, LOOKING FOR SOME LIBERATING SAIL THAT NEVER APPEARED.
UUUU.
UUUU
UUUUU
SEVEN OR EIGHT WEEKS AFTER MY LANDING, A DISASTER PUT A DIFFERENT ASPECT ON MY STRANGE SURROUNDINGS.
UUUURRAAHHHUGH
KRASH!
PRENDICK, THAT BRUTE'S LOOSE! TORE THE FETTER OUT OF THE WALL. HAVE YOU SEEN THEM? WHAT'S THE MATTER?
I WAS STANDING IN THE DOORWAY...
GOOD GOD! COME ON!

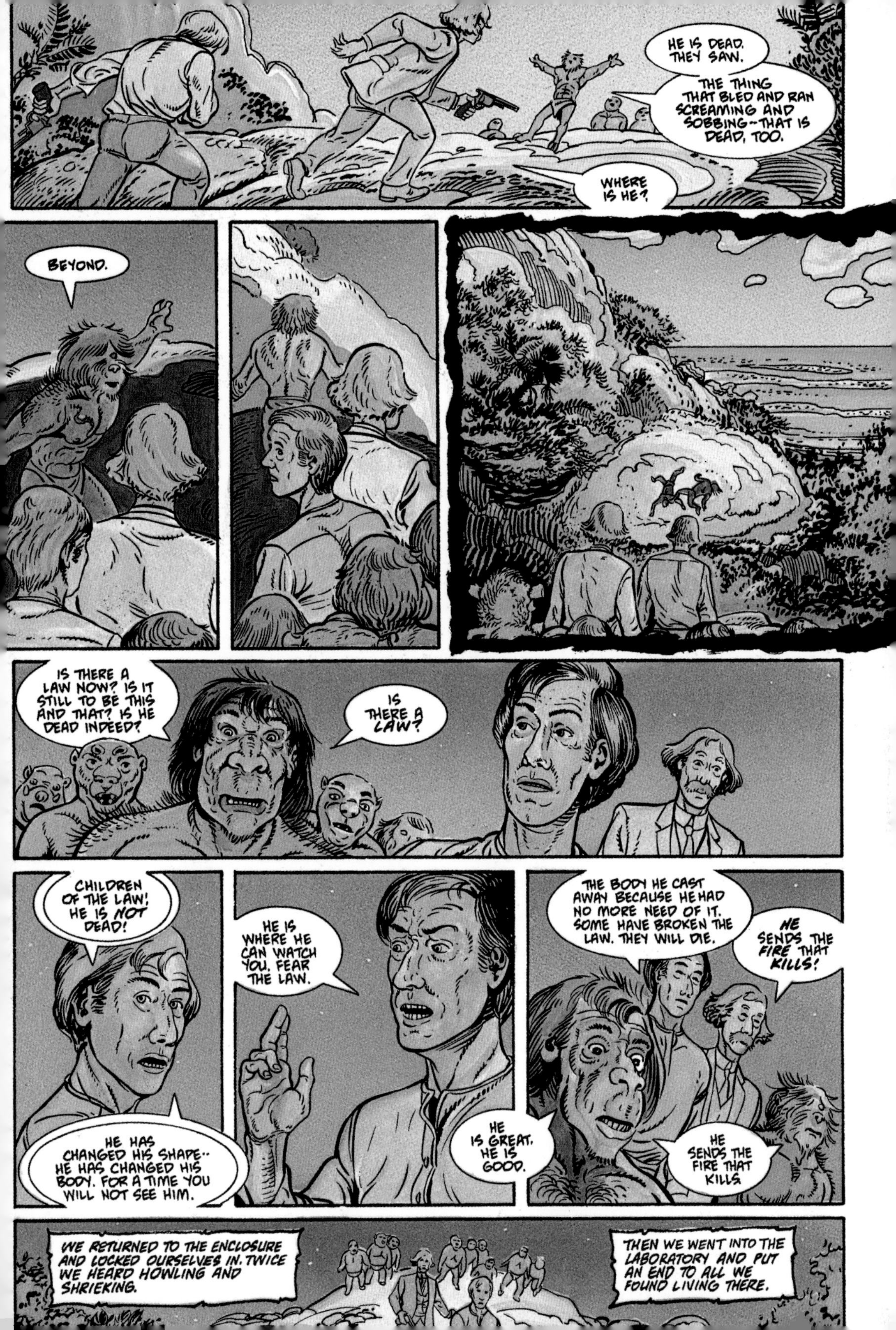

HE IS DEAD. THEY SAW.
THE THING THAT BLED AND RAN SCREAMING AND SOBBING--THAT IS DEAD, TOO.
WHERE IS HE?
BEYOND.
IS THERE A LAW NOW? IS IT STILL TO BE THIS AND THAT? IS HE DEAD INDEED?
IS THERE A LAW?
CHILDREN OF THE LAW! HE IS NOT DEAD!
HE HAS CHANGED HIS SHAPE.. HE HAS CHANGED HIS BODY. FOR A TIME YOU WILL NOT SEE HIM.
HE IS WHERE HE CAN WATCH YOU. FEAR THE LAW.
HE IS GREAT. HE IS GOOD.
THE BODY HE CAST AWAY BECAUSE HE HAD NO MORE NEED OF IT. SOME HAVE BROKEN THE LAW. THEY WILL DIE.
HE SENDS THE FIRE THAT KILLS!
HE SENDS THE FIRE THAT KILLS.
WE RETURNED TO THE ENCLOSURE AND LOCKED OURSELVES IN. TWICE WE HEARD HOWLING AND SHRIEKING.
THEN WE WENT INTO THE LABORATORY AND PUT AN END TO ALL WE FOUND LIVING THERE.

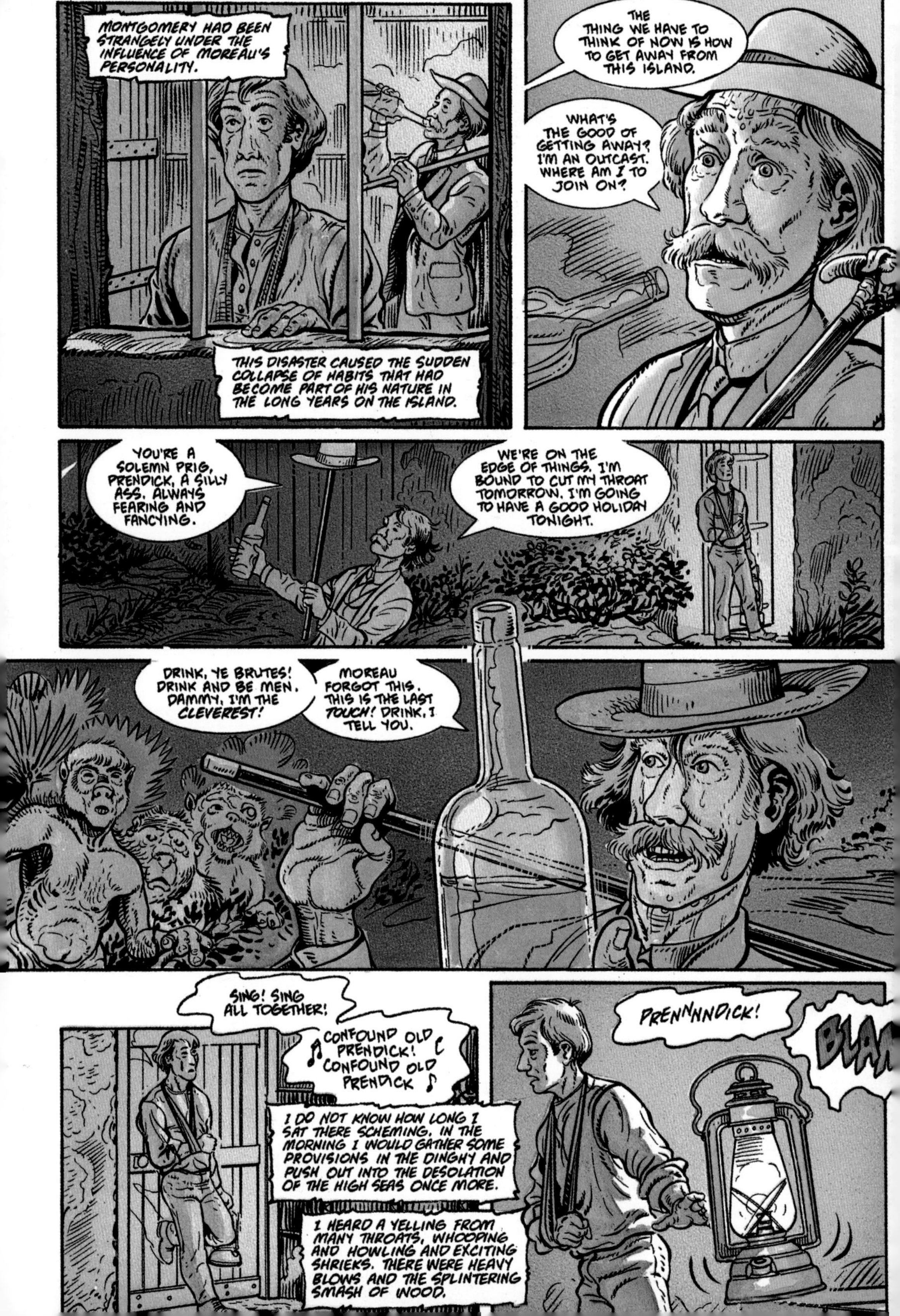
MONTGOMERY HAD BEEN STRANGELY UNDER THE INFLUENCE OF MOREAU'S PERSONALITY.
THIS DISASTER CAUSED THE SUDDEN COLLAPSE OF HABITS THAT HAD BECOME PART OF HIS NATURE IN THE LONG YEARS ON THE ISLAND.
THE THING WE HAVE TO THINK OF NOW IS HOW TO GET AWAY FROM THIS ISLAND.
WHAT'S THE GOOD OF GETTING AWAY? I'M AN OUTCAST. WHERE AM I TO JOIN ON?
YOU'RE A SOLEMN PRIG, PRENDICK, A SILLY ASS. ALWAYS FEARING AND FANCYING.
WE'RE ON THE EDGE OF THINGS. I'M BOUND TO CUT MY THROAT TOMORROW. I'M GOING TO HAVE A GOOD HOLIDAY TONIGHT.
DRINK, YE BRUTES! DRINK AND BE MEN. DAMMY, I'M THE CLEVEREST!
MOREAU FORGOT THIS. THIS IS THE LAST TOUCH! DRINK, I TELL YOU.
SING! SING ALL TOGETHER!
CONFOUND OLD PRENDICK! CONFOUND OLD PRENDICK
I DO NOT KNOW HOW LONG I SAT THERE SCHEMING. IN THE MORNING I WOULD GATHER SOME PROVISIONS IN THE DINGHY AND PUSH OUT INTO THE DESOLATION OF THE HIGH SEAS ONCE MORE.
I HEARD A YELLING FROM MANY THROATS, WHOOPING AND HOWLING AND EXCITING SHRIEKS. THERE WERE HEAVY BLOWS AND THE SPLINTERING SMASH OF WOOD.
PRENNNNDICK!
BLAM

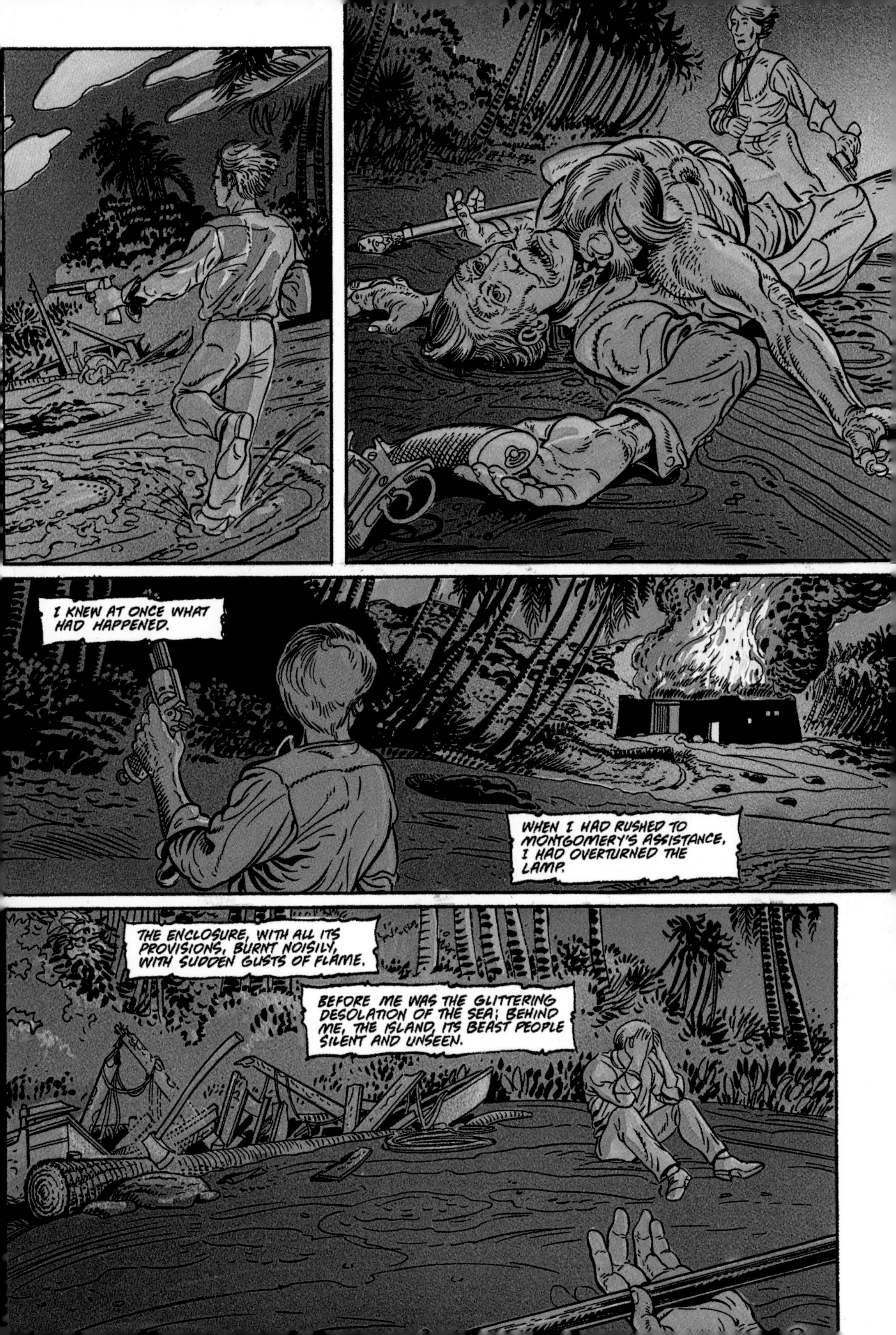
I KNEW AT ONCE WHAT HAD HAPPENED.
WHEN I HAD RUSHED TO MONTGOMERY'S ASSISTANCE, I HAD OVERTURNED THE LAMP.
THE ENCLOSURE, WITH ALL ITS PROVISIONS, BURNT NOISILY, WITH SUDDEN GUSTS OF FLAME.
BEFORE ME WAS THE GLITTERING DESOLATION OF THE SEA; BEHIND ME, THE ISLAND, ITS BEAST PEOPLE SILENT AND UNSEEN.

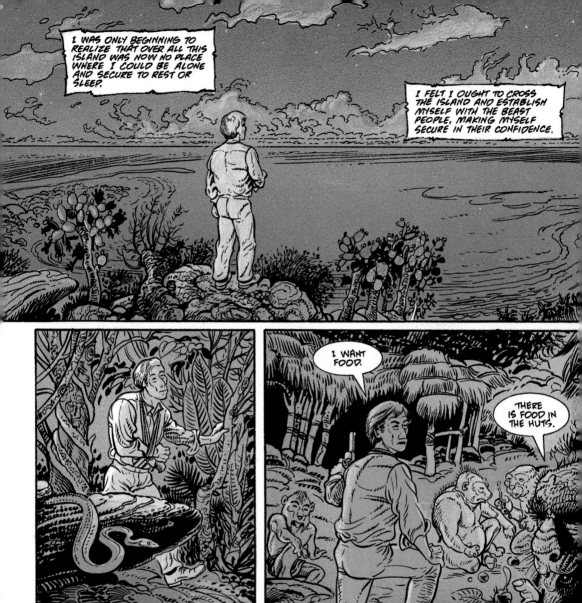

I WAS ONLY BEGINNING TO REALIZE THAT OVER ALL THIS ISLAND WAS NOW NO PLACE WHERE I COULD BE ALONE AND SECURE TO REST OR SLEEP.

I FELT I OUGHT TO CROSS THE ISLAND AND ESTABLISH MYSELF WITH THE BEAST PEOPLE, MAKING MYSELF SECURE IN THEIR CONFIDENCE.

I WANT FOOD.

THERE IS FOOD IN THE HUTS.

IN AN EMPTY HUT, I FEASTED ON SOME FRUIT. WITH MY HAND UPON MY REVOLVER, THE EXHAUSTION OF THE LAST THIRTY HOURS CLAIMED ITS OWN, AND I LET MYSELF FALL INTO A LIGHT SLUMBER.

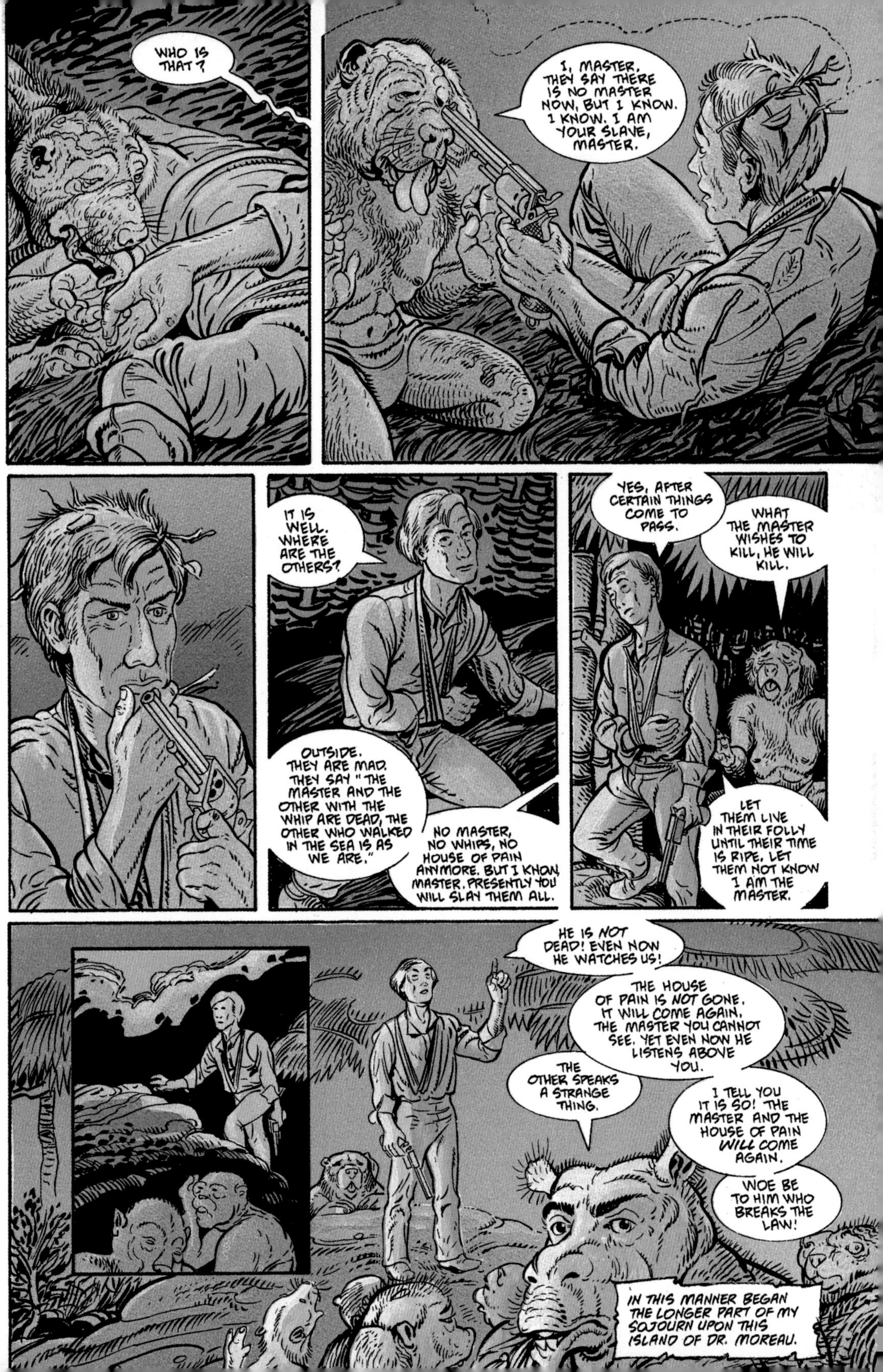
WHO IS THAT?
I, MASTER. THEY SAY THERE IS NO MASTER NOW, BUT I KNOW. I KNOW. I AM YOUR SLAVE, MASTER.
IT IS WELL. WHERE ARE THE OTHERS?
OUTSIDE. THEY ARE MAD. THEY SAY "THE MASTER AND THE OTHER WITH THE WHIP ARE DEAD, THE OTHER WHO WALKED IN THE SEA IS AS WE ARE."
NO MASTER, NO WHIPS, NO HOUSE OF PAIN ANYMORE. BUT I KNOW, MASTER. PRESENTLY YOU WILL SLAY THEM ALL.
YES, AFTER CERTAIN THINGS COME TO PASS.
WHAT THE MASTER WISHES TO KILL, HE WILL KILL.
LET THEM LIVE IN THEIR FOLLY UNTIL THEIR TIME IS RIPE. LET THEM NOT KNOW I AM THE MASTER.
HE IS NOT DEAD! EVEN NOW HE WATCHES US!
THE HOUSE OF PAIN IS NOT GONE. IT WILL COME AGAIN. THE MASTER YOU CANNOT SEE. YET EVEN NOW HE LISTENS ABOVE YOU.
THE OTHER SPEAKS A STRANGE THING.
I TELL YOU IT IS SO! THE MASTER AND THE HOUSE OF PAIN WILL COME AGAIN.
WOE BE TO HIM WHO BREAKS THE LAW!
IN THIS MANNER BEGAN THE LONGER PART OF MY SOJOURN UPON THIS ISLAND OF DR. MOREAU.

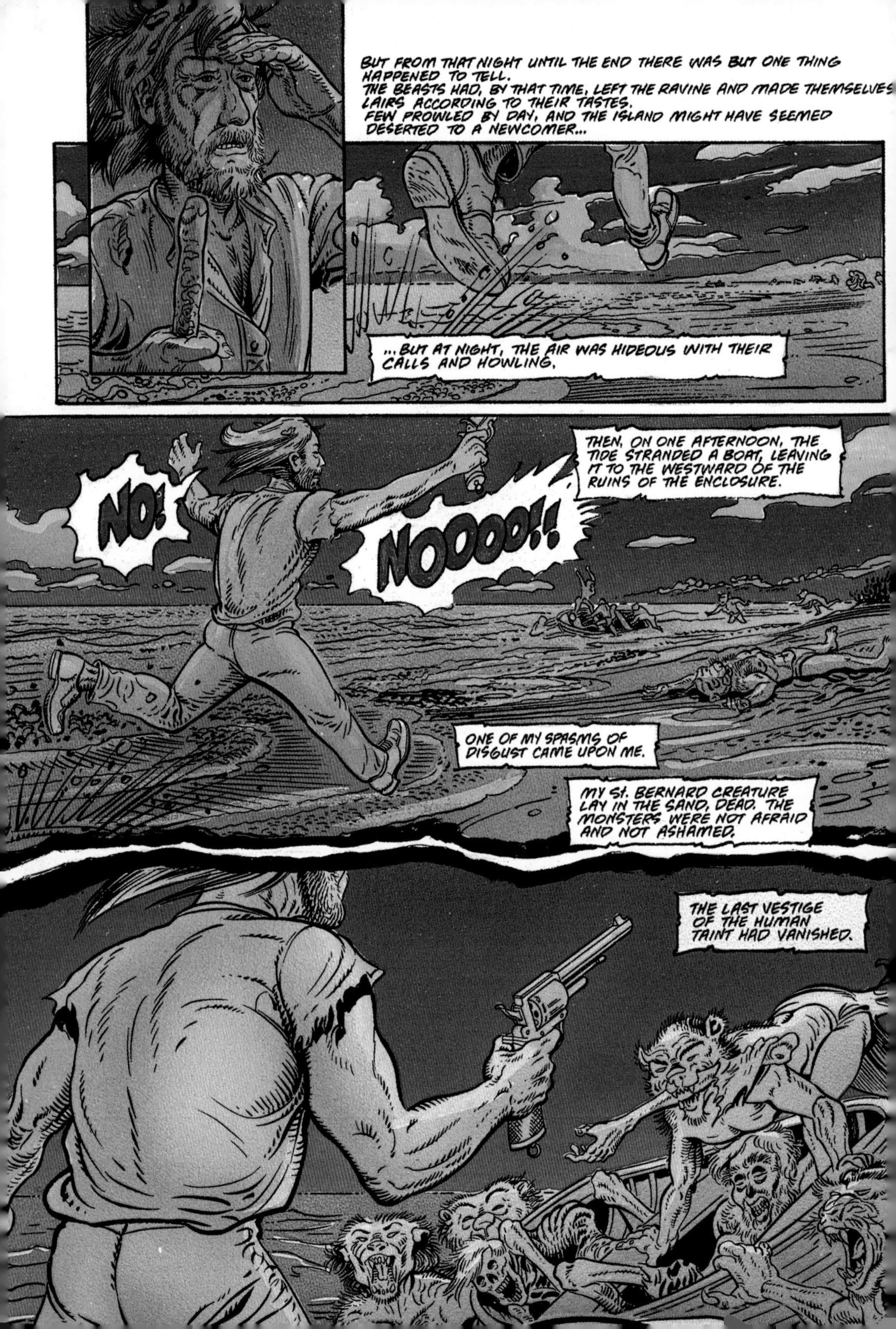
BUT FROM THAT NIGHT UNTIL THE END THERE WAS BUT ONE THING HAPPENED TO TELL.
THE BEASTS HAD, BY THAT TIME, LEFT THE RAVINE AND MADE THEMSELVES LAIRS ACCORDING TO THEIR TASTES.
FEW PROWLED BY DAY, AND THE ISLAND MIGHT HAVE SEEMED DESERTED TO A NEWCOMER...
...BUT AT NIGHT, THE AIR WAS HIDEOUS WITH THEIR CALLS AND HOWLING.
THEN, ON ONE AFTERNOON, THE TIDE STRANDED A BOAT, LEAVING IT TO THE WESTWARD OF THE RUINS OF THE ENCLOSURE.
NO!
NOOOO!!
ONE OF MY SPASMS OF DISGUST CAME UPON ME.
MY ST. BERNARD CREATURE LAY IN THE SAND, DEAD. THE MONSTERS WERE NOT AFRAID AND NOT ASHAMED.
THE LAST VESTIGE OF THE HUMAN TAINT HAD VANISHED.

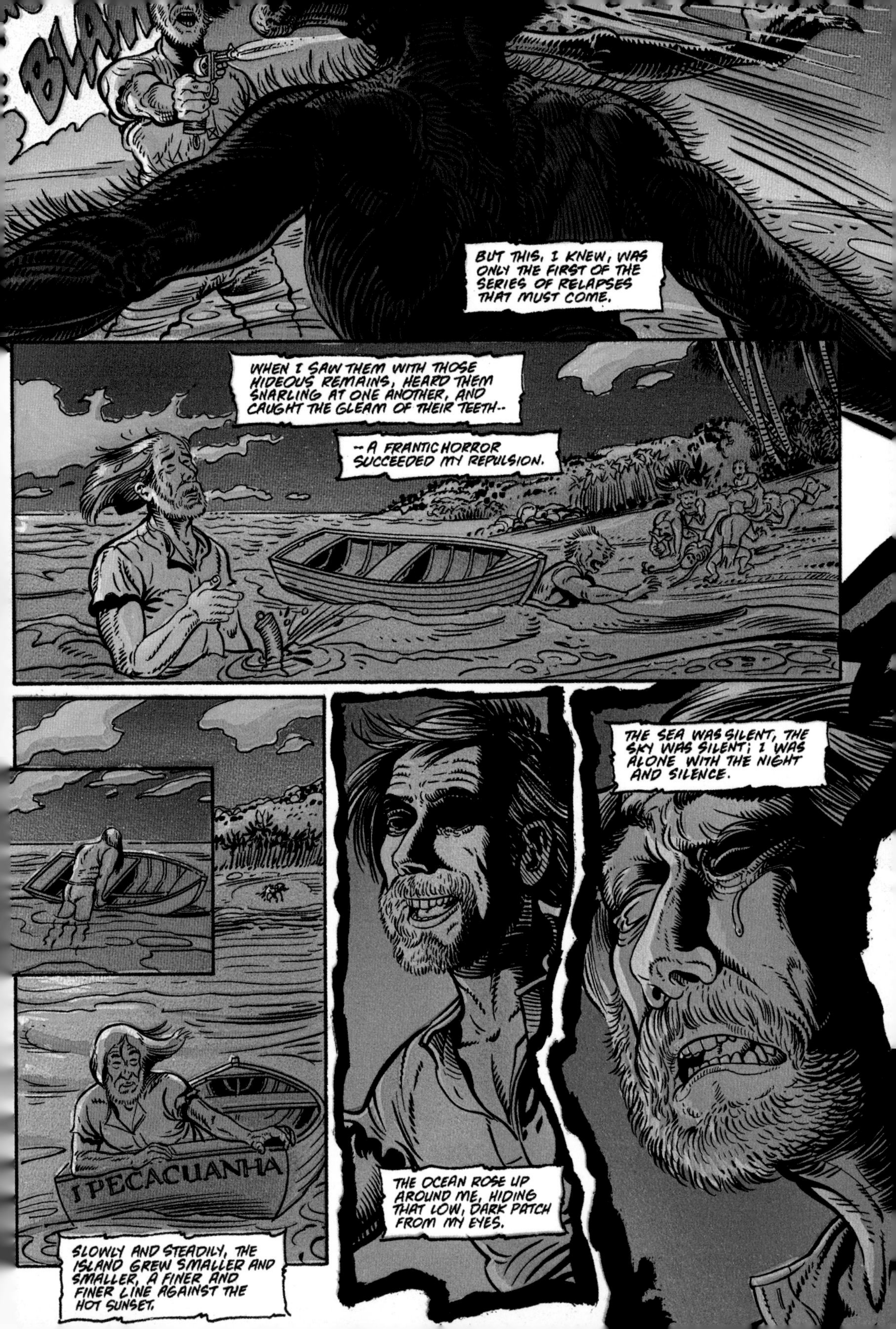
BLAM
BUT THIS, I KNEW, WAS ONLY THE FIRST OF THE SERIES OF RELAPSES THAT MUST COME.
WHEN I SAW THEM WITH THOSE HIDEOUS REMAINS, HEARD THEM SNARLING AT ONE ANOTHER, AND CAUGHT THE GLEAM OF THEIR TEETH--
--A FRANTIC HORROR SUCCEEDED MY REPULSION.
IPECACUANHA
SLOWLY AND STEADILY, THE ISLAND GREW SMALLER AND SMALLER, A FINER AND FINER LINE AGAINST THE HOT SUNSET.
THE OCEAN ROSE UP AROUND ME, HIDING THAT LOW, DARK PATCH FROM MY EYES.
THE SEA WAS SILENT, THE SKY WAS SILENT; I WAS ALONE WITH THE NIGHT AND SILENCE.

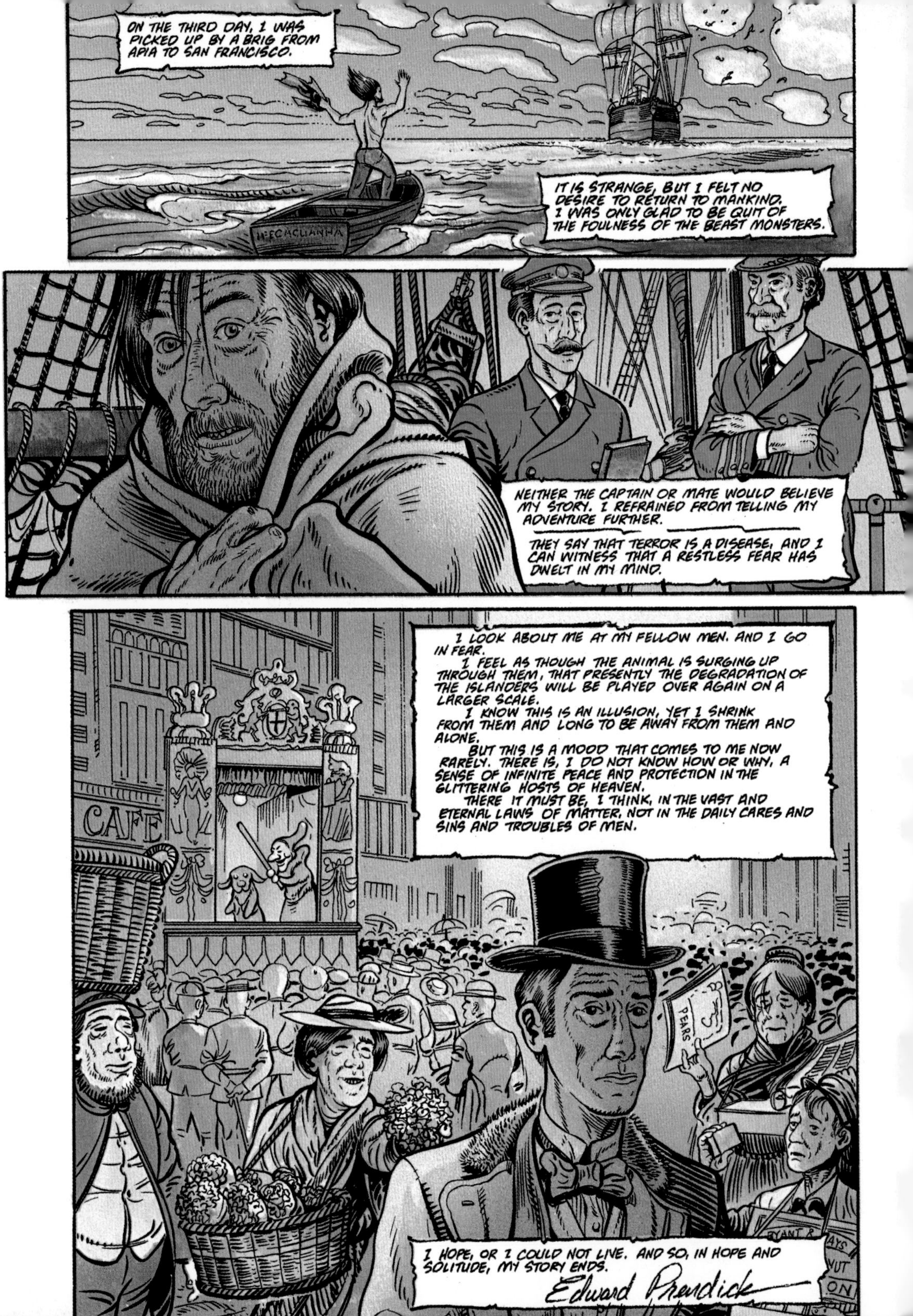
ON THE THIRD DAY, I WAS PICKED UP BY A BRIG FROM APIA TO SAN FRANCISCO.
IT IS STRANGE, BUT I FELT NO DESIRE TO RETURN TO MANKIND. I WAS ONLY GLAD TO BE QUIT OF THE FOULNESS OF THE BEAST MONSTERS.
NEITHER THE CAPTAIN OR MATE WOULD BELIEVE MY STORY. I REFRAINED FROM TELLING MY ADVENTURE FURTHER.
THEY SAY THAT TERROR IS A DISEASE, AND I CAN WITNESS THAT A RESTLESS FEAR HAS DWELT IN MY MIND.
I LOOK ABOUT ME AT MY FELLOW MEN. AND I GO IN FEAR.
I FEEL AS THOUGH THE ANIMAL IS SURGING UP THROUGH THEM, THAT PRESENTLY THE DEGRADATION OF THE ISLANDERS WILL BE PLAYED OVER AGAIN ON A LARGER SCALE.
I KNOW THIS IS AN ILLUSION, YET I SHRINK FROM THEM AND LONG TO BE AWAY FROM THEM AND ALONE.
BUT THIS IS A MOOD THAT COMES TO ME NOW RARELY. THERE IS, I DO NOT KNOW HOW OR WHY, A SENSE OF INFINITE PEACE AND PROTECTION IN THE GLITTERING HOSTS OF HEAVEN.
THERE IT MUST BE, I THINK, IN THE VAST AND ETERNAL LAWS OF MATTER, NOT IN THE DAILY CARES AND SINS AND TROUBLES OF MEN.
CAFE
PEARS
I HOPE, OR I COULD NOT LIVE. AND SO, IN HOPE AND SOLITUDE, MY STORY ENDS.
Edward Prendick

NOW THAT YOU HAVE READ THE CLASSICS Illustrated EDITION, DON'T MISS THE ADDED ENJOYMEN
OF READING THE ORIGINAL, OBTAINABLE AT YOUR SCHOOL OR PUBLIC LIBRARY

WATCH OUT FOR PAPERCUTZ ™

Welcome to the terrifying twelfth edition of CLASSICS ILLUSTRATED, featuring Steven Grant and Eric Vincent's fear-fraught adaptation of "The Island of Dr. Moreau." I'm Jim Salicrup, half-human, half-beast Editor-in-Chief of Papercutz, the proud publishers of graphic novels for all ages.

One of the many wonderful aspects of CLASSICS ILLUSTRATED, the long-running series that adapts Stories by the World's Greatest Author's into comics, is how it so enthusiastically embraces stories. Whether originally published as a prose novel, as poetry (CLASSICS ILLUS-TRATED #4 "The Raven and Other Poems"), a play (CI #5 "Hamlet," CI #10 "Cyrano de Bergerac"), or even a satirical dictionary (CI #11 "The Devil's Dictionary and Other Works"), CLASSICS ILLUSTRATED adapts these stories in all their myriad forms and shares them with you in comics form.

CLASSICS ILLUSTRATED, as originally conceived by Albert Lewis Kanter, was intended to introduce the joy of reading so-called "real" books to comicbook-obsessed children. Even though Mr. Kanter may not have accepted comics as a legitimate art form, his intentions were good— attempting to positively influence children to love literature. And it worked! Generations of children were inspired to read the actual books that the CLASSICS ILLUSTRAT-ED comics were based on. His plan may have backfired just a little, as the comic art form is so potent that for generations many schoolchildren simply read the CLASSICS ILLUSTRATED versions rather than the original novels—especially when writing their book reports.

What's so odd about the premise of trying to persuade children to read is that they are read-ing when they read comics. And it's not that difficult to get them to read prose books if the stories are compelling enough. Once kids are no longer intimidated by pages of text, they will actually enjoy reading. Whenever people say that children no longer read, books such as the Harry Potter or Twilight series come along and capture the imaginations of millions of kids (and adults), many who may have never bought a book to read on their own before.

I'll admit that when I was growing up, and started reading books such as the Dr. Seuss books and Little Golden Books, I was later a little put off by books for older readers because they lacked pictures. That's probably why I soon gravitated to comics. Words and pictures are an irresistible combination. And one of the many advantages to reading comics is that it rapidly improves your reading skills. So throughout my early academic career, I always tested as read-ing way above my grade level. In fact, in the fifth grade, I even volunteered to stay after class to help tutor other students with their reading.

Although I may have learned to read from comics, I was lucky to have many great teachers. One of my favorites was Mr. Wolf, my English teacher from J.H.S. 125 in the Bronx. Back when I attended it was a really rough school, and I don't mean academically. It was like one of those inner-city schools they always make movies about, where the students are out of con-trol. Many of the teachers who worked there were dedicated above and beyond the call of duty. Mr. Wolf was great in so many ways. First it was very clear that he cared about us. Second, he was fun—he took teaching very seriously, but that didn't mean he couldn't have fun with his class. As a result we enjoyed reading and writing; he turned all our assignments into something we wanted to do instead of something we had to do. He also supervised the school newspaper, and I can't tell you how meaningful it was to see things I wrote and drew see print. I believe his encouragement helped give me the confidence I needed to pursue my career in comics. I mean, I had to be good, because Mr. Wolf said so!

Now, all these years later, when editing CLASSICS ILLUSTRATED, I think of Mr. Wolf and the fun I had in his classes and hope that we're able to be as entertaining, educational, and inspir-ing. We hope that the stories presented here, and in the much longer adaptations in CLAS-SICS ILLUSTRATED DELUXE not only work as great graphic novels, but also inspire you to read or re-read the original books. I know, I usually do when we're assembling each new vol-ume of CLASSICS ILLUSTRATED.

Up next in CLASSICS ILLUSTRATED #13—"Ivanhoe" by Sir Walter Scott, adapted by Mark Wayne Harris and Ray Lago. Don't miss it!

Let us know what you think of CLASSICS ILLUSTRATED. Either email me at salicrup@papercutz.com or send a letter to CLASSICS ILLUSTRATED, Papercutz, 40 Exchange Place, Suite 1308, New York, NY 10005.

Thanks,

CLASSICS ILLUSTRATED DELUXE
GRAPHIC NOVELS FROM PAPERCUTZ

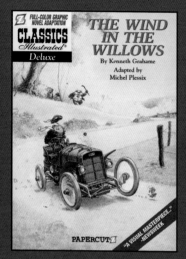

#1 "The Wind
In The Willows"

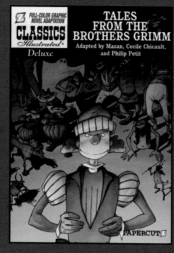

#2 "Tales From
The Brothers Grimm"

#3 "Frankenstein"

#4 "The Adventures
of Tom Sawyer"

#5 "Treasure Island"

CLASSICS ILLUSTRATED DELUXE graphic novels are available for $13.95 each in paperback and $17.95 in hardcover. Please add $4.00 for postage and handling for the first book, add $1.00 for each additional book. MC, Visa, Amex accepted or make check payable to NBM Publishing.
Send to: Papercutz, 1200 Rte. 523, Flemington, NJ 08822 • 1-800-886-1223

WWW.PAPERCUTZ.COM

PAPERCUTZ ASKS

CLASSICS ILLUSTRATED WRITER

STEVEN GRANT

A FEW QUESTIONS...

Steven Grant was born in Madison, Wisconsin, in 1953, and graduated from the University of Wisconsin. Grant's comics credits include *Twilight Man, Whisper, Punisher* and *Life of Pope John Paul II*. The former editor-in-chief of the *Velvet Light Trap Review of Cinema*, Grant has written music criticism for *Trouser Press*, and has contributed to several books on popular culture, including *Close-Ups* and *The Rock Yearbook*. Grant has also written a variety of widely praised young-adult adventure novels.

Recently, Papercutz Associate Editor Michael Petranek emailed a few questions to the writer responsible for the adaptations of "Hamlet" (CLASSICS ILLUSTRATED #5), "The Count of Monte Cristo" (CI #8), and "The Island of Dr. Moreau" – Steven Grant. Here are those questions, and Steven's informative responses...

MICHAEL PETRANEK: What is your process when adapting a classic novel to a script for comics? Is it the same for each, or do you approach each work differently?

STEVEN GRANT: It's been awhile since I've done it, but 1) Reread at least a couple times, so everything's fresh in your mind. 2) Outline the major plot points, character developments and focal dialogue. 3) Break the action down across however many pages you have to work with, and see how many pages you have for each point/development/dialogue chunk. That's where it gets tricky, because then you have to become a cruel editor, seeing what you can eliminate while still keeping the story intact, and what you can compress to fit. The idea is to keep the end result as close to

the source material as possible, but, especially when you're adapting a lengthy novel to, say, 44 pages of comics, it can be like trying to stuff three suitcases worth of clothes into one suitcase. You also need to allow for stylistic complexity of the original work and other variables. Since you're ending up with comics, you also need to note the most visual elements of the story, because those will make a more visually appealing comicbook, but when it came down to visuals or content, I usually try to err on the side of content. The ultimate step is really to just dive in and keep bashing things into shape. When you get into it, systems are useless, and you have to do whatever the book requires. It's the difference between training in boot camp and getting dumped in the middle of a firefight. The prep is useful, but ultimately you do what you have to.

MP: Papercutz has published three CLASSICS ILLUSTRATED graphic novels you've adapted, "Hamlet," "The Count of Monte Cristo," and "The Island of Dr. Moreau." How was adapting each one of these works different from the other?

SG: As the shortest, "Dr. Moreau" was the easiest of the lot and required the least amount of excising to fit. As events in the book were somewhat repetitive by nature, it was also easier to compress action, combining two scenes into one here and there while losing very little. "Hamlet" and "Count" are much longer works, and required a lot to be stripped down. I think I was maybe able to bring in a full third of Shakespeare's play, much as I hated to touch it. But there are a lot of asides, subplots and secondary character bits that had to go by the wayside. It was a matter of saving and highlighting the most key moments, made somewhat easier by the play having a very strong core story thruline. "Count" was the toughest of the lot, since it is all plot. Everything dovetails into everything else, everyone knows each other in some way. And the original's some 800 pages long! So everything had to be very, very compressed. Some reviewer said the adaptation reads like a runaway train, and that's probably pretty accurate. There really wasn't another choice, and I praise artist Dan Spiegle for holding the whole thing together.

MP: If you could adapt any play or novel for comics, what would it be?

SG: When I was first contacted about CLASSICS ILLUSTRATED, they asked what classic novel I most wanted to adapt, and right off the top of my head, I said Thomas Pynchon's "Gravity's Rainbow." They said they meant something a little more widely considered a classic. I thought about it a few seconds, then tentatively offered, "The Naked Lunch," by William S. Burroughs. They basically hung up on me. Only later did I realize they meant books in public domain. "The Island Of Dr. Moreau" was one I really wanted to do, since I love the ending, it's very creepy, but everyone who adapts the book leaves that off and I wanted to get it in there for a change. The Shakespeare play I really wanted to do was Macbeth, but it was spoken for. I'd love to do all the extant Greek plays: Aeschylus, Euripides, Sophocles. I'd like to do various myth cycles, like Celtic myths, and modern adult works. But I think a new sort of visual language would have to be developed to equal the stylistic developments in modern fiction and we're not there yet. It's a wide open wilderness, though, with tons of possibilities. Adaptations into comics form have only scratched the surface of what could be done.

MP: What writers did you look up to growing up, in comics or otherwise?

SG: It's funny. I know I read a lot when I was a kid, but I don't remember specifically what I read. The earliest books I remember reading were "Charlotte's Web" and Isaac Asimov's "Pebble in the Sky," which I loved, but I don't think I ever read anything else by

Tom Mandrake Illustrated Steven Grant's adaptation of "Hamlet" (below). Dan Spiegle illustrated "The Count of Monte Cristo" (opposite)

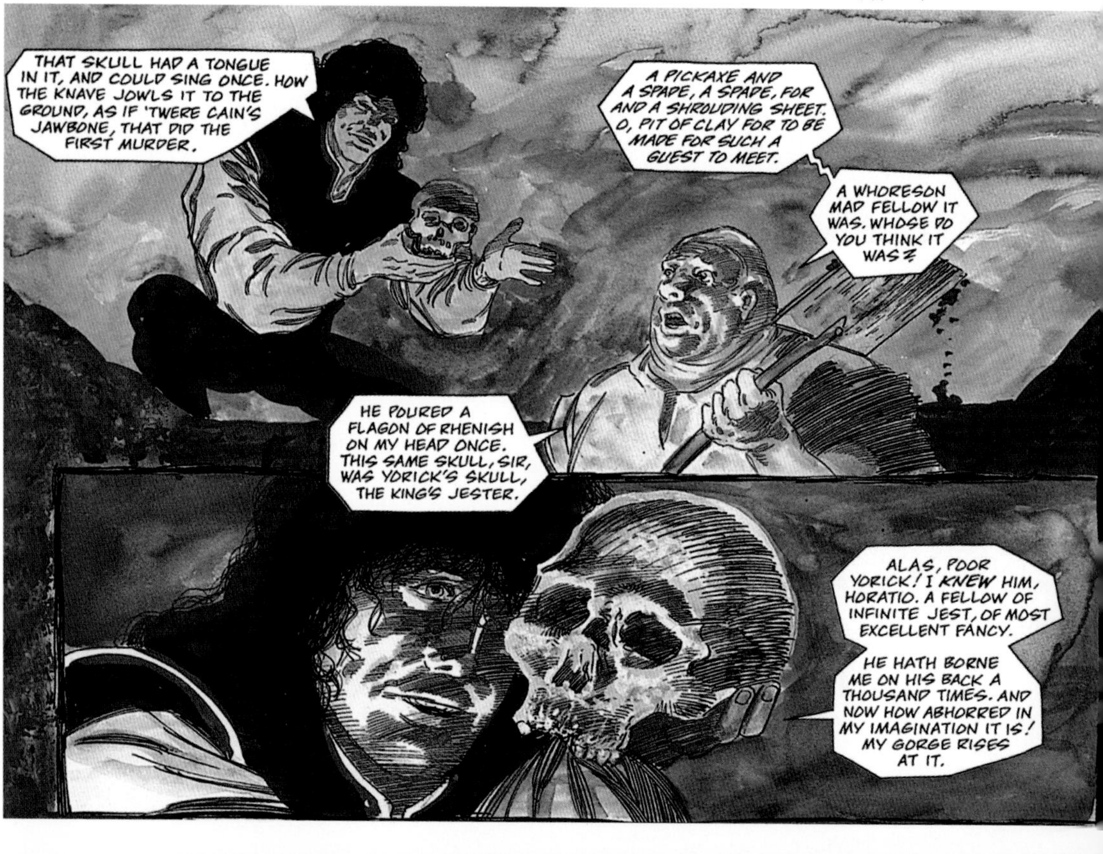
THAT SKULL HAD A TONGUE IN IT, AND COULD SING ONCE. HOW THE KNAVE JOWLS IT TO THE GROUND, AS IF 'TWERE CAIN'S JAWBONE, THAT DID THE FIRST MURDER.
A PICKAXE AND A SPADE, A SPADE, FOR AND A SHROUDING SHEET. O, PIT OF CLAY FOR TO BE MADE FOR SUCH A GUEST TO MEET.
A WHORESON MAD FELLOW IT WAS. WHOSE DO YOU THINK IT WAS?
HE POURED A FLAGON OF RHENISH ON MY HEAD ONCE. THIS SAME SKULL, SIR, WAS YORICK'S SKULL, THE KING'S JESTER.
ALAS, POOR YORICK! I KNEW HIM, HORATIO. A FELLOW OF INFINITE JEST, OF MOST EXCELLENT FANCY.
HE HATH BORNE ME ON HIS BACK A THOUSAND TIMES. AND NOW HOW ABHORRED IN MY IMAGINATION IT IS! MY GORGE RISES AT IT.

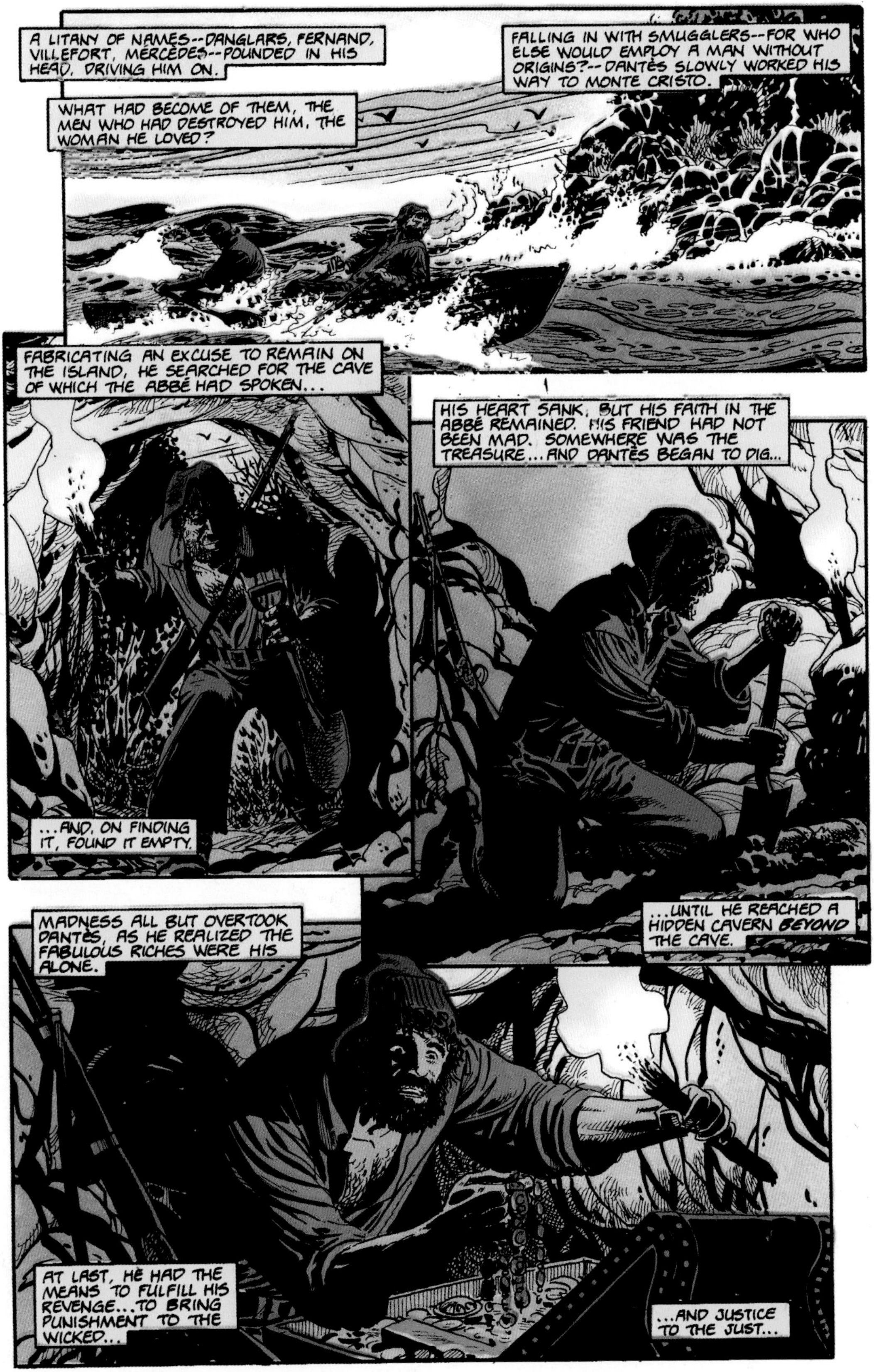
A LITANY OF NAMES--DANGLARS, FERNAND, VILLEFORT, MERCÉDÈS--POUNDED IN HIS HEAD, DRIVING HIM ON.
WHAT HAD BECOME OF THEM, THE MEN WHO HAD DESTROYED HIM, THE WOMAN HE LOVED?
FALLING IN WITH SMUGGLERS--FOR WHO ELSE WOULD EMPLOY A MAN WITHOUT ORIGINS?--DANTÈS SLOWLY WORKED HIS WAY TO MONTE CRISTO.
FABRICATING AN EXCUSE TO REMAIN ON THE ISLAND, HE SEARCHED FOR THE CAVE OF WHICH THE ABBÉ HAD SPOKEN...
...AND, ON FINDING IT, FOUND IT EMPTY.
HIS HEART SANK, BUT HIS FAITH IN THE ABBÉ REMAINED. HIS FRIEND HAD NOT BEEN MAD. SOMEWHERE WAS THE TREASURE...AND DANTÈS BEGAN TO DIG...
...UNTIL HE REACHED A HIDDEN CAVERN *BEYOND* THE CAVE.
MADNESS ALL BUT OVERTOOK DANTÈS, AS HE REALIZED THE FABULOUS RICHES WERE HIS ALONE.
AT LAST, HE HAD THE MEANS TO FULFILL HIS REVENGE...TO BRING PUNISHMENT TO THE WICKED...
...AND JUSTICE TO THE JUST...

those writers. I know I had a book of King Arthur stories that I read over and over, and my mother had a book of Greek myths I also reread incessantly. Pretty much I read whatever landed in front of me, anything from Daniel Defoe to John Fowles. By high school I was reading a lot of science fiction, especially writers such as Michael Moorcock, Thomas Disch, and Harlan Ellison, and my tastes ran strongly toward what was then known as "British New Wave," and I read a lot of plays and experimental fiction. Some spy novels, like “The Spy Who Came In From The Cold,” and one by a guy named Jack Hunter that has always stuck with me, called “One Of Us Works For Them.” Very influential in my thinking about fiction; stumbled across it a couple years ago and tried to read it, and the writing turns out to be awful. Good plot, though. I don't think you mind awful writing when you're a kid. But what you read isn't as important as that you read a lot, and try lots of different things.

MP: Are there any new projects you're writing that you'd like to tell us about?
SG: I haven't done a lot of comics lately, as I've been working on a lot of media stuff, and what I've done recently, like a horror novel for Vertigo, doesn't seem to be comin out anytime soon. My most recent publishe work is *Odysseus The Rebel*, from Big Head Press (www.bigheadpress.com), that's not so much an adaptation of *The Odyssey* as a reinterpretation that I've wanted to do for some time. The basic story's all there, but I took liberties with the theme and dialogue. I'm currently working on another horror graphic novel for Arcane Studios (www.arcanacomics.com). And I'm going of next week to discuss a raft of new projects a Boom! Studios. Bad timing on my part, eh?

MP: Thanks, for answering my questions, Steven, and all of us at Papercutz wish you continued success with all your projects.

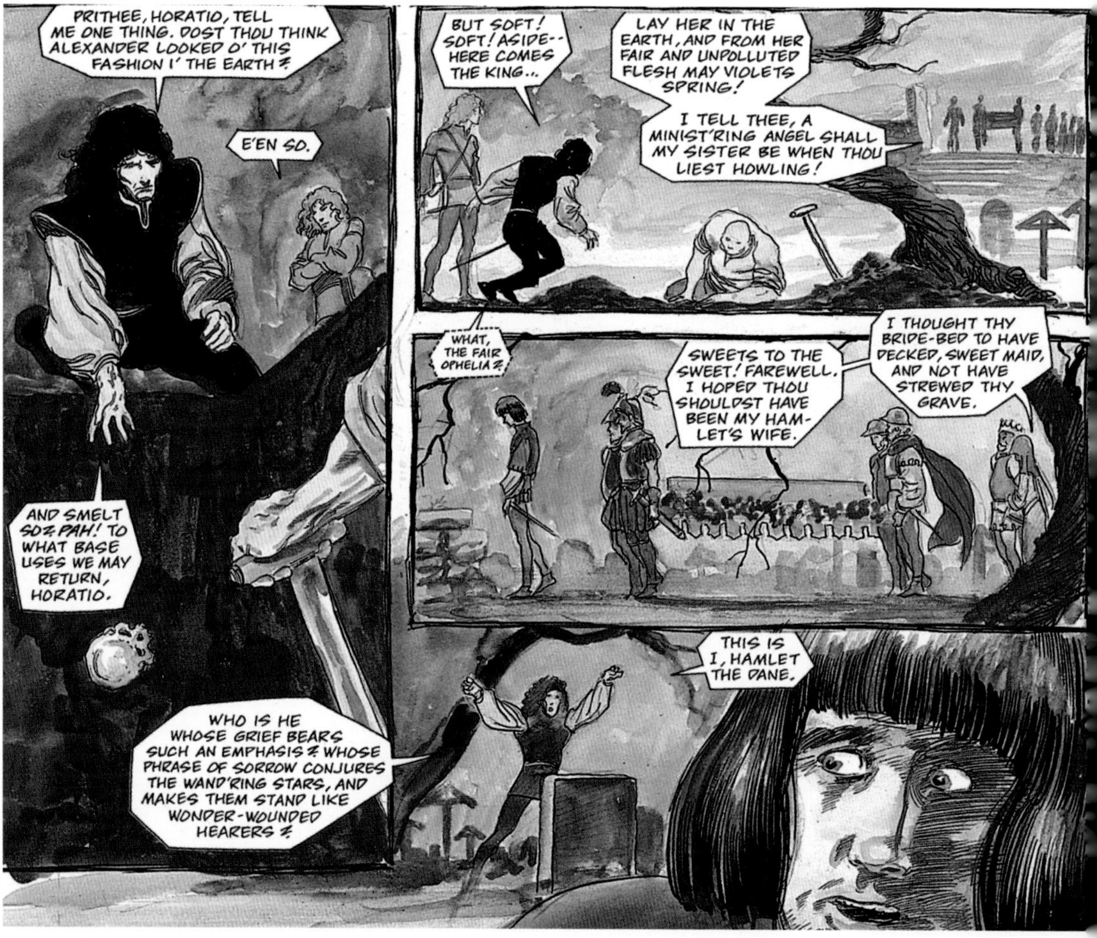
PRITHEE, HORATIO, TELL ME ONE THING. DOST THOU THINK ALEXANDER LOOKED O' THIS FASHION I' THE EARTH?
E'EN SO.
AND SMELT SO? PAH! TO WHAT BASE USES WE MAY RETURN, HORATIO.
BUT SOFT! SOFT! ASIDE-- HERE COMES THE KING...
LAY HER IN THE EARTH, AND FROM HER FAIR AND UNPOLLUTED FLESH MAY VIOLETS SPRING!
I TELL THEE, A MINIST'RING ANGEL SHALL MY SISTER BE WHEN THOU LIEST HOWLING!
WHAT, THE FAIR OPHELIA?
SWEETS TO THE SWEET! FAREWELL. I HOPED THOU SHOULDST HAVE BEEN MY HAMLET'S WIFE.
I THOUGHT THY BRIDE-BED TO HAVE DECKED, SWEET MAID, AND NOT HAVE STREWED THY GRAVE.
WHO IS HE WHOSE GRIEF BEARS SUCH AN EMPHASIS? WHOSE PHRASE OF SORROW CONJURES THE WAND'RING STARS, AND MAKES THEM STAND LIKE WONDER-WOUNDED HEARERS?
THIS IS I, HAMLET THE DANE.

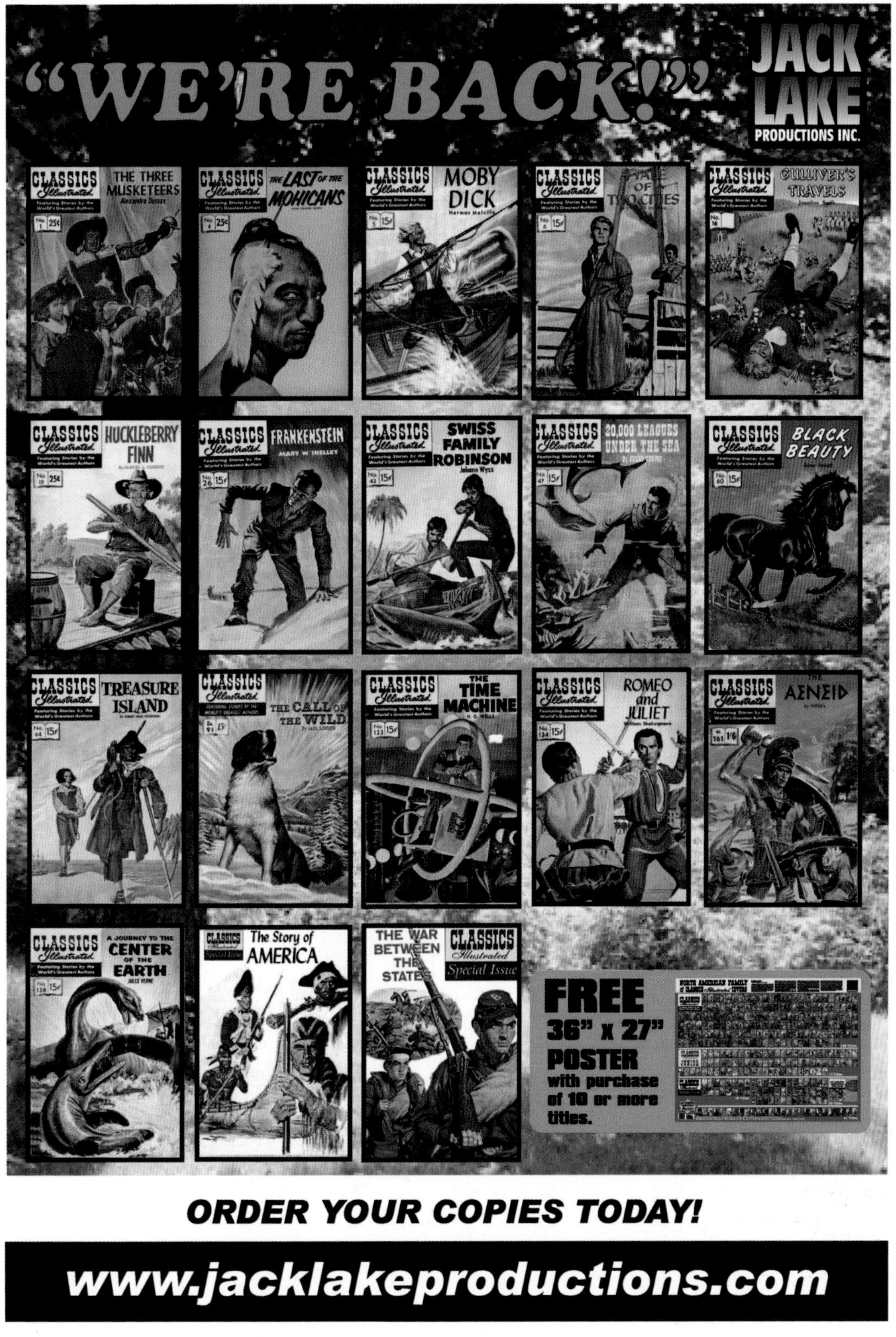
"WE'RE BACK!"
JACK LAKE
PRODUCTIONS INC.
CLASSICS Illustrated THE THREE MUSKETEERS Alexandre Dumas No. 1 25¢
CLASSICS Illustrated THE LAST OF THE MOHICANS No. 4 25¢
CLASSICS Illustrated MOBY DICK Herman Melville No. 5 15¢
CLASSICS Illustrated A TALE OF TWO CITIES No. 6 15¢
CLASSICS Illustrated GULLIVER'S TRAVELS No. 16
CLASSICS Illustrated HUCKLEBERRY FINN No. 19 25¢
CLASSICS Illustrated FRANKENSTEIN MARY W. SHELLEY No. 26 15¢
CLASSICS Illustrated SWISS FAMILY ROBINSON Johann Wyss No. 42 15¢
CLASSICS Illustrated 20,000 LEAGUES UNDER THE SEA No. 47 15¢
CLASSICS Illustrated BLACK BEAUTY No. 60 15¢
CLASSICS Illustrated TREASURE ISLAND No. 64 15¢
CLASSICS Illustrated THE CALL OF THE WILD No. 91 15¢
CLASSICS Illustrated THE TIME MACHINE H. G. WELLS No. 133 15¢
CLASSICS Illustrated ROMEO and JULIET William Shakespeare No. 134 15¢
CLASSICS Illustrated THE AENEID by VIRGIL No. 161 1/6
CLASSICS Illustrated A JOURNEY TO THE CENTER OF THE EARTH JULES VERNE No. 138 15¢
CLASSICS Illustrated Special Issue The Story of AMERICA
THE WAR BETWEEN THE STATES CLASSICS Illustrated Special Issue
FREE
36" x 27"
POSTER
with purchase of 10 or more titles.

H.G. WELLS & ERIC VINCENT

H.G. WELLS was born in Bromley, Kent, England, on September 21, 1866, the son of an unsuccessful small businessman and a domestic servant. In 1884, Wells won a scholarship to the University of London, where he was strongly influenced by Thomas Huxley, the famed Darwinian biologist. Wells's early novel, *The Time Machine* (1895), reflected his lifelong fascination with science. Described as a "scientific romance," *The Time Machine* was a popular success, and contributed greatly to the critical acceptance of literature that blended fiction with scientific theory and predictions. Although he was preceded by the French fantasist Jules Verne, Wells – whose works combined conjecture, adventure, satire, and social and political theories – was considered the first great serious writer of what came to be known as science fiction. In quick succession, he wrote *The Island of Dr. Moreau* (1896), *The Invisible Man* (1897), *The War of the Worlds* (1899), and *The First Men in the Moon* (1901). In 1903, Wells joined England's socialist Fabian Society; impatient and independent, he soon left after a disagreement with his sponsor, the playwright George Bernard Shaw. After the turn of the century, Wells produced a number of widely read novels that mirrored his interest in feminism, socialism, and nationalism. Those works, such as *Tono-Bungay* (1909), and *The New Machiavelli* (1911), earned Wells a role as an influential social commentator. Although twice-wed, Wells was an outspoken critic of conventional marriage; his one child, a son, was born out of wedlock in 1914 to the novelist Rebecca West. With the publication of the massive *The Outline of History* (1920), and its briefer offspring, *A Short History of the World* (1922), Wells's following continued to grow. Throughout his life, Wells was greatly concerned about the survival of society, and depicted his dreams of an ideal world in books like *Men Like Gods* (1923), and *The Shape of Things to Come* (1933); some of his visions included world government by supermen, and a new religion based on physics. His later years, though, were marked by fear that technological advances were outdistancing intellectual, moral, and social development. *Mind at the End of Its Tether* (1945), Wells's last work, was a despairing prediction of humanity's future. Wells died in 1946, not long after the first use of atomic weapons.

ERIC VINCENT was born in Gainesville, Florida, in 1953, and graduated from the University of Southwestern Louisiana. Vincent has spent 15 years in advertising, as an art director, illustrator, writer, director and producer. He has published his own magazine, *Cerberus*, and has worked as a newspaper illustrator and cartoonist. Vincent has illustrated four children's books. One of those, *Clovis Crawfish and the Orphan Zo-Zo*, won the 1984 Children's Choice Award; another, *Henry Hamilton, Graduate Ghost*, was adapted into a television special. Vincent's comics credits include the critically acclaimed *Alien Fire*.